This book belongs to:

Esther

A TREASURY
of
Animal Stories

For Robin and William – HW
For Dan – JAD

www.hollywebbanimalstories.com

STRIPES PUBLISHING
An imprint of Little Tiger Press
1 The Coda Centre, 189 Munster Road, London SW6 6AW

A paperback original
First published in Great Britain in 2014

ISBN: 978-1-84715-459-0

A CIP catalogue record for this book is available from the British Library.

Printed and bound in China.

STP/1800/0050/0614

2 4 6 8 10 9 7 5 3 1

A TREASURY
of
Animal Stories

From best-selling author
HOLLY WEBB

stripes

CONTENTS

Dear Reader,

Here is a collection of my short stories about some very special animals — from hedgehogs to penguins. I have always loved animals and my own pets have inspired lots of my characters, including some that are in this book.

I hope you enjoy reading these stories as much as I enjoyed writing them!

Lots of love,

Holly x

THE STRANGEST SLEEPOVER

"But I don't want to share my bedroom!" Izzy glared crossly at her mum, her fingernails digging into her palms. Her dachshund puppy, Trixie, gave her a worried look. She didn't like it when Izzy was upset. Her ears flattened down, and she tucked her tail between her legs, glancing between Izzy and the safety of her basket. She wasn't sure which to run to.

Izzy gulped, trying not to cry, and made herself speak in a calmer voice. "It's OK,

Trixie. Shhhh. I didn't mean to scare you."

Trixie scuttled towards her, and nuzzled gratefully at Izzy's hands.

"Izzy, I don't see why this is such a problem!" Her mum was staring at her, frowning in a confused sort of way. "You *like* Charley!"

"You got on really well," her dad put in, nodding.

"Yes, for one day, at Auntie Kat's wedding! That's not the same as having her in my bedroom for two weeks!" Izzy shook her head. How could they possibly think she'd be happy about it? She *had* got on well with her cousin Charley when they'd been bridesmaids together – it had been fun, having someone her own age to giggle with during all the boring speeches.

The cousins lived so far apart that they'd only met a couple of times before, and Izzy hadn't really remembered Charley. It had felt like meeting someone new. Izzy had even camped in Charley's room at the hotel, like a sleepover. But this was … different. Charley's mum, her aunt Lucy, was going on a training course for work – and Charley was coming to stay with them.

"Her stuff will be all over the place," she muttered. She knew it sounded a bit feeble, but she couldn't explain it any better. Her room was just for her – and Trixie, of course.

Izzy had only had her puppy for two months, but she could hardly remember what it was like, not having a dog. Trixie had a smart new basket in the kitchen, which she used for daytime naps. (Mum said she spent most of her life asleep, but Izzy was sure that Trixie was tired all the time because her legs were so short. She walked about three times as many steps as everybody else did, trotting along to keep up.) But at night Trixie slept on a blanket spread over the end of Izzy's bed. Izzy had learned not to wriggle about in the night, after the time she was woken up at

midnight by a panicked little yelp as Trixie
fell off the end of the bed.

"Anyway, Charley might not like animals,"
she pointed out. "She might not want to share
a room with me and Trixie."

Her mum and dad exchanged glances,
and Izzy stared at them suspiciously. "What?
What is it?"

"Well, we were going to suggest that
Trixie slept in the kitchen, just while
Charley's staying with us."

"She actually doesn't like dogs?" Izzy
asked disgustedly.

"No," Izzy's dad shook his head. "I think
Charley's very fond of animals. That's the
problem, you see. She's bringing Sammy with
her."

Izzy frowned. Sammy? Did Charley have a dog, too? Or maybe Sammy was a cat? "Is Charley bringing a cat?" she asked, frowning worriedly. Trixie really wasn't going to like that. Or rather, she would like it, a lot too much. It would be two weeks of war…

"Er, no…" Mum gave a little shiver, and made a face.

"Actually, Sammy's a rat," Dad explained. "I think Charley got him about the same time you got Trixie. And it's a bit difficult to find a petsitter for a rat, apparently. So while Charley's staying with us, Sammy's going to have to come, too."

Izzy's mum shook her head. "Aunt Lucy suggested we could keep him in the kitchen!"

Izzy giggled, even though she was cross.

Her mum was not good with mice and rats. Or spiders, or snakes… "You could keep him on the counter."

"Don't, Izzy!" Her mum shuddered. "I know it's stupid, and they're lovely pets really, but I just couldn't… Or the living room. I'm afraid he'll have to go in your room. But you like rats, don't you?"

Izzy sighed. It was true that she'd always liked looking at the rats in the pet shop. She loved animals, and she'd been desperate for any sort of pet. She loved the rats' sparkling eyes, and she didn't mind their pink tails the way Mum did. But that didn't mean she wanted to share a room with one!

"Hi, Izzy! This is so exciting!"

Charley came racing up the path to the front door, with Aunt Lucy hurrying behind her. Izzy tried to smile, and look pleased to see them. Mum had explained to her that it wasn't fair on Charley to sulk – Charley didn't have much choice about having to spend two weeks of her summer holiday away from her mum and all her friends. Izzy had reluctantly decided that was true, and she'd promised she'd try to be nice.

"Oh, Izzy, is this your dog? You're so lucky! She's gorgeous!" Charley crouched down to admire Trixie, who was peering round Izzy's ankles.

"What's her name?"

"Trixie," Izzy admitted, feeling a bit better

about her cousin, now she obviously had good taste in dogs.

"She's beautiful," Charley breathed, holding out her hand for Trixie to sniff.

Trixie licked the girl's fingers, and sniffed at her thoughtfully. She smelled like Izzy, somehow, and her voice was like Izzy's, too. Soft, and friendly.

"You're so lucky having a dog," Charley said, giggling as Trixie's tongue tickled her fingers. "I can't have one – Mum's out at work, and I'm at school, so a dog would get really lonely. I've got Sammy instead, though, and he's fab. Did my mum tell you about him?"

Izzy nodded. "Your rat? Is he in the car?"

"Yes, the cage is on the back seat. I think he's a bit confused – he's hiding in his sleeping pod. He's been sticking his nose out every so often when we stop at lights, but then we start moving again, and he pops back inside." Charley patted Trixie, and stood up. "I'll get him. Can you help me carry his cage out of the car?" Sammy's massive cage was taking up most of the back seat. As far as Izzy could see, though, it was completely empty of rat.

She couldn't even see him in his bedroom.

"Thanks for letting me keep him in your room," Charley said as they edged the cage up the stairs between the pair of them. "You're sure you don't mind?" She peered down over the top of the cage at Izzy, and saw her frown. "Oh! You do mind!"

Izzy tried to smile, and say it was fine, but it didn't work very well, and Charley was looking hurt.

"Look, let's just get to the top of the stairs before we drop it," Izzy muttered, pushing the cage a little, so that Charley had to stumble up another step. "This is my room. I cleared the stuff off my desk." *Because Mum made me,* she didn't add. "We can put his cage there."

Charley gently let go of the cage, and peered in, looking for Sammy. But he was still hiding in his bedroom after the bumpy ride up the stairs. "What's the matter?" she asked, turning to Izzy. "Don't you like rats? Your mum doesn't, I can tell, even though she's pretending Sammy's OK. They're really friendly, you know, if you keep handling them, and they don't smell, not if you clean out the cage properly."

"Oh no, it isn't that – I think they're cute.

It's just weird, having someone sharing my room," Izzy blurted out.

She could have kicked herself when she saw the hurt look on Charley's face.

"I mean, it'll be fun," she added quickly. "It's just that I'll miss Trixie. She's got to sleep downstairs because Sammy's going to be in here."

"Oh…" Charley's face fell even further. "I suppose she might try and chase Sammy. I didn't think about that. Sorry," she added, in a very small voice.

All at once, Izzy discovered that she wasn't cross any more. All the things her mum and dad had been saying about how this was much harder for Charley than it was for her made sense, and she felt mean.

Her bedroom didn't matter all that much,
not when Charley looked so miserable and
lonely. And she would make it up to Trixie
somehow. Extra treats. Super-long walks.
Charley could come, too.

"It's fine," she said quickly, giving Charley
a hug. "I was just being stupid. Oh, look! Is
that him?"

A black nose was sticking out of the
sleeping pod, a black nose and a set of
immensely long black
whiskers. The two girls
held their breath, and
after a few seconds,
the rest of Sammy
appeared. Glittering
eyes, sleek black and

white fur, and that long, strong tail.

"Gosh, he's bigger than I thought he would be."

"I know, and he's still only young," Charley said proudly. "I think he's going to be massive when he's fully grown. Do you want to meet him properly? He can be a teensy bit shy with new people, but if you feed him some apple he'll love you forever."

"Shall I get an apple from downstairs?" Izzy suggested hopefully.

There was a scurry of paws on the landing, and the two girls gasped.

"Trixie! She's followed us. It takes her ages to get up the stairs – they're huge steps for her, because her legs are still so little." Izzy dived to the door, and grabbed Trixie just as she popped her head round. "Sorry, sweetie, you can't come in."

Trixie wriggled in her arms, wondering what the strange new smell was. Not another dog, she was sure, but *something* – and in Izzy's room. *Her room.* She sniffed, confused but curious, and wriggled even harder.

"I'd better take her downstairs," Izzy said, sighing, and carrying Trixie over to the door. "I'll put her in the kitchen and come back up with some apple, OK?"

The Strangest Sleepover

"Are you all right?" Izzy whispered to Charley, later that night. Her cousin was sleeping on a fold-out sleepover bed, squished up next to hers. It was almost dark in her bedroom now, and Sammy seemed to have gone to sleep at last. He'd been pottering around his cage, rustling his bedding, and nibbling his seed mix. It had all sounded oddly loud to Izzy, who was only used to the gentle breathing of a dog.

It had been a fun day – after they'd waved off Aunt Lucy, they'd taken Trixie for a walk. Because there were two of them, Mum had actually let them go without her. She'd lent Izzy her phone just in case, and spent about ten minutes getting them to promise to be sensible and not cross any roads, while Trixie jumped up and down and tried to chew her lead to bits. They'd gone all through the woods, giggling, and racing Trixie, and it had been fab. Then Trixie had collapsed in her basket, so they'd gossiped and played with Sammy upstairs.

But somehow, towards bedtime, both girls had grown quieter. Izzy was worrying about Trixie, and whether she'd be miserable downstairs on her own. And she guessed Charley was feeling homesick.

"Mmmmm. I'm OK…" But Charley didn't sound very sure.

"Are you missing your mum?"

"A bit," Charley snuffled, and Izzy wondered if she were trying not to cry. She had looked a bit teary when Aunt Lucy had driven away that morning.

"Do you want me to get my mum?" she suggested doubtfully.

"No…" Izzy heard Charley gulp. "Can I get Sammy out and cuddle him?" she whispered. "He's very good. He won't poo on your floor or anything like that. Sometimes I let him sleep in a shoebox on the corner of my bed."

Izzy hesitated. She wasn't totally sure about a free-range rat in her bedroom. But Charley sounded really upset. "All right," she muttered. "But you won't let him climb on my bed, will you? I mean, I do love him, but…"

"Promise," Charley agreed gratefully. She got up and opened the cage, hooking out a warm, sleepy ball of fur.

Izzy could just see her snuggling Sammy
up against her neck. Sighing, she turned
over and buried her face on her pillow. She
missed feeling Trixie snuggled up next
to her feet, even though it was nice to be
able to wriggle about. Trixie had been so
confused when Izzy went to say goodnight

to her just before bed. She'd sat in her basket, staring after them as they closed the kitchen door, and then she'd whined, for ages. Izzy guessed she must be asleep now. She was quiet, anyway.

But Trixie wasn't asleep. She didn't understand why Izzy had left her in the kitchen, and she had no intention of staying there. She belonged in Izzy's room, whatever else was up there. Ever since Izzy's mum and dad had gone up to bed, Trixie had been pacing backwards and forwards in front of the door, trying to find a way to follow Izzy upstairs.

She sniffed grumpily at the crack around the kitchen door, and nudged at it with her nose. She'd never been able to open it before, but Izzy's dad hadn't pulled it tightly closed, and now it moved, just very slightly. Trixie's tail stuck out straight behind her, quivering with excitement. It had definitely moved!

Cautiously, Trixie hooked her polished black claws into the space between the door and the frame and pulled, skittering out of the way as the door swung slowly open. She was free!

Upstairs, Izzy twitched, and sighed, and fell more deeply asleep, and Charley wriggled, and rolled over with a little snore. She nuzzled into her pillow, and Sammy, forgotten, slipped out from under her chin, and buried himself in a nest-like hollow further down her duvet. Then he stared towards the door, whiskers twitching nervously. He could hear scrabbling, and panting dog-breaths, and the thump of a solid little body heaving itself up step after step. He backed away a little, huddling against Charley, as footsteps pattered along the landing. And then a pointed muzzle peered curiously round the door, and came sniffing and snuffling towards him.

Sammy let out a worried squeak.

Trixie trotted up to the sleeping bag and sniffed again. She could see something soft and furry moving in the shadows, and she still wasn't quite sure about the smell. But Izzy was fast asleep in the bed. Trixie could hear her deep, slow breathing.

The other girl definitely reminded her of Izzy. And *she* didn't mind this small furry creature. She was stroking it in her sleep, her hand cupped round its back.

Trixie sighed wearily. It had been very hard getting up the stairs. And she definitely couldn't climb up on to Izzy's bed. Izzy usually lifted her. So she would have to make do with just being close to Izzy. She'd sleep with the girl who smelled a bit like her. And the furry thing, which was still watching her cautiously.

Trixie climbed on to the sleeping bag, and gave it a friendly sniff.

Sammy let his whiskers droop a little, and sniffed back. Charley kept wriggling in her sleep and the dog was curling up nicely further towards the end of the sleeping bag. The dog looked warm and comfortable to curl up with. He pattered down the sleeping bag to Trixie, and nuzzled hopefully at her nose.

The puppy stared at him in surprise, but she was too sleepy to complain. If Izzy wanted the rat thing in her room, that was up to her. She wriggled herself round the small ball of fur protectively, and went to sleep.

And that was how Izzy and Charley found them, when they woke up the next morning. A smooth ball of dachshund, curled up asleep behind Charley's knees, with a bright-eyed, whiskery face peeping out over her back.

"Charley!" Izzy whispered, leaning down from her bed, and gently shaking her cousin's shoulder. "Charley, look!"

Charley yawned, and wriggled out of her sleeping bag a bit, and looked down where Izzy was pointing. "What? Oh!"

"They've made friends! They had a sleepover," Izzy told her, with a smile. "Just like us."

RATS

Rats have a bad reputation for being dirty, but they can actually make very clean and friendly pets!

FACTFILE

Animal Group:
Mammal (Rodent)

Size:
25cm from tip of nose to tip of tail to tip of nose

Colour:
Brown

Personality:
Shy and hardworking

Food:
Fruit, worms and insects (yuck!)

Did You Know?

A group of rats is called a mischief.

Male rats are known as bucks, females as does and babies can either be pups or kittens.

A rat can survive longer than a camel without drinking water.

Famous Rats

Remy From the film *Ratatouille*, this determined rat is obsessed with delicious food. Together with his human friend Linguini, he cooks up some amazing dishes and eventually fulfils his dream of becoming a chef!

Scabbers The pet rat belonging to Ron Weasley in the "Harry Potter" series by J.K. Rowling. Simply a rather scruffy pet for the first few books, Scabbers actually turns out to be an evil wizard in disguise!

Did You Know?

Holly's favourite food is chocolate.

Holly has three sons, including twins.

Holly's favourite film is *The Sound of Music*.

When Holly was little, a cuddly white bear named Polar was her favourite toy. Polar inspired Holly to write her wintry book *The Snow Bear*.

Holly is terrified of spiders.

42

Holly wrote her first book while travelling by train to and from her job as an editor in London. She often had to write sitting on the floor.

Holly's birthday is on 4th February.

Holly's favourite colours are purple and green.

Holly's favourite subject at school was Ancient Greek — she loves Greek myths.

Holly enjoys making jewellery and painting.

THE KITTEN TREE

"Come on, girls! Emily, what are you bringing that for?"

"I want to show him to Grandma." Five-year-old Emily had her favourite present, a two-metre-long cuddly snake called George, wrapped round her neck like a fat and dangerous scarf.

"Emily, we're walking to Grandma's." Molly knelt down by her little sister. "George is heavy. You'll get tired carrying him. And he might get dirty if you drop him."

"I want to show George to Grandma!" Emily's face was going red. Her family knew the signs, so Molly shrugged. "I'll help her carry him."

Mum nodded. No one wanted an Emily tantrum on Christmas Day. She could go on for ages, and the girls' grandma was expecting them. "All right, if we must."

Dad took Emily's hand, and tucked a box of crackers under his arm. "Ready, everyone? Come on, Emily, let's go and see if Grandma's got a present for you."

Emily nodded happily, and started

to pull him towards the door. "Maybe she's got me another snake!" she was squeaking excitedly.

Mum and Molly looked at each other and sighed.

Ruby the kitten stretched and yawned luxuriously. She was draped along the back of the sofa, snoozing after a big lunch. It had been particularly good, with turkey, and gravy. Emily had tried to feed her something called Christmas pudding as well, but Molly had stopped her. Ruby hadn't minded. It hadn't smelled like her kind of thing anyway. She could still smell turkey though.

Mmmm… She wondered if they'd put it all away in the fridge?

Suddenly Ruby sat bolt upright. They'd all gone for mince pies at Grandma's house! This was her moment. For the last two weeks, Ruby had been desperate to investigate the Christmas tree. It was so clearly meant for kittens to climb, but no one seemed to want her to. They kept shooing her away. Ruby leaped delicately down from the sofa, and padded over to the tree, whiskers twitching in excitement. She sat in front of it, curling her tail round her paws thoughtfully. Where should she start? She reached out and batted a silver bauble, which swung deliciously. She batted it again, a little harder, but this time it came off, thudding on to the floor. Ruby peered down at it, wondering if it would bounce up again. She jumped back, fur bristling, when she saw another cat inside, one with a strange wide face, enormous eyes and silvery tabby stripes like hers. She hissed, and the other cat made a hissy face, but no noise came out. It seemed well and truly stuck in there. Good. This was *her* house.

Ruby had been hoping not to leave any evidence of her climb, so she scooted the bauble, and the trespassing cat, under the sofa.

The cat intruder had been a little bit of a shock. Obviously, for an expedition up a Christmas tree, a kitten's nerves needed to be in top working order. Ruby took up a guarding position on the sofa arm, just in case that cat tried coming out again, and settled down for a good wash.

Ten minutes later, Ruby was ready to try again. She peeked under the sofa, but the other cat was still underneath, and didn't seem to see her. Her tail held proudly high, Ruby strutted over to the Christmas tree. If there were any more cats hiding in it, they had better watch out! This time, she didn't

let herself get distracted by swinging baubles
– she was looking for the way up. Ever since
the girls' father had carried the Christmas
tree into the house, Ruby had wanted to get
inside it and explore, and when they'd added
tinsel and twinkly lights and a fairy doll on
the top, it just got even more interesting.

Ruby stood up with her paws on the big,
gold-painted pot that Mum and Molly had
made. She shook her ears twitchily as a few
pine needles pattered down
around her. There were
a lot of branches, but
none of them looked
very secure. She
tested one lightly
with a paw.

More pine needles whispered down. Hmmm. Ruby was only a few months old, but she'd learned a lot in that time, and one of the most important things she knew was that a Big Leap was often the answer. She jumped for the biggest branch she could see, scrabbling her soft, shiny little claws at it. But it wasn't there! Or, actually, the branch was there, it was Ruby that wasn't. She was on the floor, blinking dazedly up at the tree. The twinkly lights seemed to be shimmering even more than before, and moving about. And there might have been another cat in one of those baubles, laughing at her.

Ruby was forced to consider something that she hadn't thought of before. Was it possible that the tree did not want her to climb it? No, that was silly. She knew trees. There were trees in her garden, and she climbed those. They didn't mind. But then this was an indoor tree. Maybe indoor trees were fussy? Ruby stood up and glared at the tree. It was in her house, therefore it was her tree. That was obvious. So it was going to be climbed, whether it liked it or not. Perhaps not a Big Leap, though that method hadn't been quite as successful as she had hoped.

Cautiously, she hooked some tinsel with one claw, and pulled. The tinsel sagged, but not too much. It wasn't going to be much good to climb on though – too thin and straggly. And it stuck to her claws – uugh! Ruby shook her paw hard, and the tangled tinsel yanked away from the tree and managed to wrap itself round her several times. It was alive! And it was attacking her!

Ruby and the tinsel wrestled for a good five minutes until she was happy that it was thoroughly beaten. Then she stepped daintily out of the nest of sparkly shredded silver bits, and had another reassuring wash, paying particular attention to her poor paws. Once they were back to their old selves, Ruby turned again to the tree, a determined gleam in her eyes. This time, she meant business. It was now clear to her that she'd been distracted by silly things like tinsel and feathery branches. Trees had trunks, and that was what she needed. She would wriggle her way up the trunk.

A very small doubt had begun to grow in the back of Ruby's mind. It was all very well getting up the tree, but what was she going to do when she was there? Was there any point to all this? Might it not be better to go back to the sofa and have a bit more of a sleep instead? Ruby squashed the doubt firmly back down. She had been planning to climb the Christmas tree for ages. She didn't need a reason. It was just a kitten thing.

This was clearly a sneaky tree, so Ruby needed to be sneaky, too. She settled into her hunting pose, tummy to the carpet, and crept round to the back of the tree. Ruby had done lots of hunting. She'd never actually caught anything, but that wasn't important. The tree was going to get a big shock. She'd be at the top before it knew what had hit it. She launched herself on to the pot, and swarmed as fast as she could up the tree trunk, her eyes like slits and her ears laid back. The pine needles were showering all around her, but she wasn't going to stop.

Amazingly enough, it worked. Ruby was quite surprised, although, of course, she pretended she'd known she could do it all along. She clung to the top of the tree, peering triumphantly round the fairy doll's sparkly skirt. It was wonderful! She could see everything: the sofa, the table, Molly and Emily's piles of new toys and books. The floor … which seemed to be an awfully long way down. Ruby tightened her grip on the tree. She was still wobbling, though.

The tree was wobbling her. In fact, one might even say it was swaying. The floor definitely was a very long way down. Down wasn't something that Ruby had really planned for.

What would happen if she just let go? Ruby tried, but her claws wouldn't do it. They seemed to think it was Not A Good Idea. Could she go back the same way she had come? Nose first? Ruby leaned over to look, and the top of the tree came too, and the fairy doll. Then they all bounced back again, rather hard.

When the tree had stopped swinging – almost – Ruby took a deep breath. Maybe down wasn't a good place to be at the moment. She would stay with up, until…

Aha! There were noises in the hallway.
Ruby tried to look as relaxed as anyone could
while clinging for dear life to the top of a
Christmas tree.

"Ruby!" Molly called. "We're back! Do you
want some tea? More turkey? Ruby, where
are you?"

"Mrowl!" Ruby spat back crossly. Of course she wanted tea, but she was a bit busy at the top of a tree at the moment, actually…

Molly popped her head round the door and gasped. Then she raced back into the hallway, while Ruby hissed furiously after her. "Where are you going? Get me down!"

Molly was back seconds later with Dad running behind. "I knew we should have shut her in the kitchen," he groaned. "I wonder how long she's been up there. Come on, you silly cat." And he reached up and grabbed Ruby round the middle. It wasn't very dignified, but she decided not to complain this time. At least Molly made a proper fuss of her, stroking her till Ruby closed her eyes and purred happily. After a little more petting, she opened her eyes again, staring thoughtfully over Molly's shoulder at the curtains. She hadn't really noticed them before.

They looked as though they might be fun to climb. . .

How I Became a Writer

When I do school visits, one question I'm often asked is whether I wanted to be an author as a child. Everyone seems surprised when I say no — I enjoyed writing, but I really really loved to read, and I did it a lot. My original career choice was to be a librarian, so I could just sit in a room full of books all day.

I did think about being an archaeologist for a while, as one of my favourite books was a children's history book on the Egyptians. Then I discovered that archaeology was a bit muddy, so I changed my mind.

As well as loving books, I was rather animal-obsessed. We had a cat, Rosie, and I spent a lot of time chasing her around so I could try to dress her in my dolls' clothes. Obviously I don't recommend this! She was very tolerant, but I did usually end up with scratched hands.

Me with Rosie, my first pet

Rosie

Over the years, other pets our family had were: a chocolate-coloured mouse called Truffle who spent most of his life in a box on the Aga recovering from constant colds, twelve gerbils, two hamsters and two dogs. Not everything in my animal stories actually happened to us, but our animals did seem to have quite a lot of adventures...

I like big cats, too!

My mother and I created the idea behind *Lost in the Snow*, the first animal book I wrote, very early on. I think I must only have been about four or five, so it's quite hard to remember the details, but we had a game we played, telling a heart-rending story about a lost kitten — with sound effects supplied by me. I still make a very good mee-ooo, mee-ooo sad kitten noise...

Me today

THE CHRISTMAS VISITOR

"Lucy! Lucy!"

Lucy looked up from her book. She was huddled into the little armchair in the corner of the living room, next to the radiator, and she had a fleecy blanket wrapped round her. It was freezing, even inside the house. Everyone said it was going to snow soon, and she wished it would. At the moment, the days were just cold and dark. It wasn't making the holidays feel very Christmassy.

The living-room door slammed open, and

her little brother stood there, panting. He was practically round. When he'd said he wanted to go and play in the garden, Mum had insisted on him wearing a fleece under his big coat, and two scarves.

"What is it? Is it snowing?" Lucy asked hopefully, turning to peer out of the window. But the sky was still a dark streaky grey, and no snow was falling.

"No. I've found something. Come and see!" Sam was so excited, he was actually dancing up and down.

"Outside?" Lucy shuddered. "No, thank you."

"You have to!" Sam trundled up to her armchair, snatching the book and snapping it closed. "Come on, Lucy, he might go! You'll be sorry if you miss him!"

Lucy frowned. "Miss who? Oh, Sam, it's
not another spider, is it? Ha-ha, very funny.
Lucy doesn't like spiders. Old joke."

Sam shook his head. "No. Actually, I think
he might eat spiders. So you should really like
him. Come on!"

"A frog?" Lucy asked doubtfully. She
couldn't think of anything else that might eat
spiders. Maybe a bird…

"Of course not a frog!" Sam sighed. "I'm going back out, I want to watch him." He stomped away, and Lucy stared after him. He had sounded very excited…

Shaking her head, she hurried into the hallway to find her coat and her snowboots. Then she went out of the back door, rubbing her gloved hands together as the cold air bit into her.

The frost was still thick and silvery on the grass, even though it was the middle of the afternoon. And there was actually an icicle hanging off the dripping garden tap! What on earth was she doing out here, instead of snuggled up in the warm?

"You came! He's here, Lucy, look!" Sam turned round from the little wooden shelter by the garden shed. Dad had made it, to store the logs for the wood-burning stove. Next to the logs was a tatty old wicker basket, full of thin twigs and dry leaves for kindling.

"What is it?" Lucy stayed a safe distance away. She really didn't like fetching logs for the stove. She always seemed to get jumped on by the world's most enormous spiders. They liked the dry, woody little space.

"I'm not quite sure!" Sam sounded excited, but then he added, in a worried sort of voice, "But whatever animal he is, I don't think he's very well, Lucy. He's a bit wobbly."

Forgetting about the spiders, Lucy hurried over. Sam was crouched down in front of the wood store, and at his feet was a brownish, spiky ball.

"A hedgehog!" Lucy leaned down to look closer, and saw a soft little brown snout, and two dark, glittering eyes. The hedgehog was waving his nose from side to side, as though he was confused.

"Shouldn't he be asleep?" Lucy said. "Don't hedgehogs hibernate?"

Sam looked up at her, frowning. He didn't know what hibernate meant.

"They sleep through the cold winter. Because there isn't much for them to eat, I think," said Lucy. "No slugs around when it's snowing."

"They eat slugs?" Sam looked disgusted. "Yuck!" Then his face crumpled. "But I woke him up! I didn't mean to, but I wanted to build a track for my cars with the wood, and

"Raisins? Really? OK…"
Lucy found some and scattered
them artistically over the top.
"Did you find out
anything else?"

"Only that he
might want to go
and find somewhere
else to sleep, now that he's been disturbed,"
Mum told her.

"Oh no… He doesn't look like he's up to
that, Mum. And I'm worried about him going
next door – what about Sukey and Billy?"

Mum nodded. "I see what you mean. Well,
if we put really nice food down for him, maybe
he'll stay put, and go back to his old bed."

Lucy sighed. "It's the best we can do, isn't it?

And maybe warn Mara next door to watch out for him whenever she lets Sukey and Billy out. Do you think that's enough food?"

Mum smiled. "Enough for a hedgehog Christmas party. Come on."

"He's still here," Sam called in a sort of loud whisper as he saw Mum and Lucy coming down the garden path.

"It's even colder now it's getting dark." Lucy shivered. "Poor hedgehog."

The hedgehog was hunched up in front of the wood store, looking sleepy. But he heard them coming and looked up, backing away from them a little.

"It's OK," Lucy whispered, putting the food down. She put it close to the pile of logs, hoping that he'd eat, and then go back and curl up behind them. She glanced round at Mum. "If he's sleeping here, we'll have to use some different wood for the stove! Or we'll keep waking him up!"

Mum nodded. "It's OK. We can put some logs in the garage instead."

"Look! He's going to eat it!" Sam said excitedly, and then clapped his hand over his mouth as the hedgehog looked up from the peanut butter again. "Sorry!" he whispered.

Lucy giggled. "He's got it on his nose!"

He had. He was obviously hungry – he wolfed the peanut butter down with loud grunts, and then started on the chicken.

"We need to make sure he's cosy…" Lucy
muttered. And then she grinned. "Back in a
minute!" She dashed into the house, and then
came back out to the garden, trailing a long,
pink scarf.

"What's that for?" Mum asked, frowning.

"To help him keep warm! It said on the

website about them needing extra warmth in their nests when it's really cold, didn't it? It's OK, Mum. It's the one Gran knitted me last Christmas. You know she's knitting another one for this year, she always does!"

Mum sighed. "You're right. Orange and purple stripes, this year's one."

Lucy made a face. "Well, then I think it's OK to give this one to a good cause, don't you?" She picked out a few of the logs from one side of the wood store, and she and Sam arranged them into a sort of pyramid behind the kindling basket, making sure it was really solid. They didn't want the logs to fall on their hedgehog. Then she tucked in the scarf to make a snuggly nest underneath.

"Let's step back a bit," Mum suggested. "If he does want to go in, he might not do it when he knows we're watching."

They headed a safe distance away, peering round the corner of Sam's slide.

The hedgehog licked the plate clean of the last chickeny bits, and sniffed the air thoughtfully.

Lucy laughed. "He looks like Grandad, deciding which armchair to sleep in after Sunday lunch! He really does!"

It was true. The hedgehog looked very full, and very sleepy. If he'd had a knitted waistcoat on (Gran liked to knit those, too) he would have been a dead ringer for Grandad. He wandered a few steps towards the wood store, and gave Lucy and Sam's new nest a cautious sniff.

"He likes it!" Sam whispered excitedly as the hedgehog stepped a little closer.

And he did. He went all the way in, padding down the scarf, and making sleepy little snuffling noises.

"We should leave him to go to sleep," Lucy murmured.

"Can we go and see him later?" Sam asked hopefully as they headed back to the house. "Can we make sure he's OK?"

Mum shook her head. "We probably shouldn't. He needs to get back to sleep."

Lucy frowned. "It's only two days till Christmas. Maybe we could go and see him again on Christmas morning? If we promise to leave him alone till then?"

Sam sighed. "I suppose so." Then he turned round, beaming. "Lucy, look!" He pointed up at the sky, which was a dark purply blue now, with a few stars glittering.

Fat snowflakes were mixing with the stars, and twirling down towards them. Lucy laughed, and stretched out her hands, catching the sparkling flakes. Then she gave Sam a hug. "It's lucky you found him when you did, Sam. What if Dad had gone to get some logs, and the hedgehog had woken up and gone wandering out in a snowstorm? Now we know to keep him safe."

Sam nodded. "We can look after him – he's our special Christmas visitor!"

HEDGEHOGS

When these little creatures burrow
for food under hedges they make
grunting noises, like pigs!

FACTFILE

Animal Group:
Mammal

Size:
25cm from tip of nose to tip of tail

Colour:
Brown

Personality:
Shy and hardworking

Food:
Fruit, worms and insects (yuck!)

Did You Know?

The name for a baby hedgehog is a hoglet.

Hedgehogs have about 5000 spines. Each spine lasts for about a year before dropping out and a new spine grows in its place.

Hedgehogs are nocturnal — they spend the daytime sleeping and are most active at night.

Famous Hedgehogs

Mrs Tiggy-winkle This hardworking character from Beatrix Potter's *The Tale of Mrs Tiggy-winkle* was based on the author's own pet.

Sonic This adventurous video game character has bright blue spines, can run at supersonic speeds and attacks enemies by curling up into a ball in a "spin attack".

93

Holly and her Fans

Holly loves meeting the children who read her books and can often be found visiting schools, bookshops and festivals across the UK.

At events, Holly reads extracts of her books out loud and often talks about the inspiration behind her favourite characters. Holly sometimes brings along Polar the polar bear, her favourite toy from childhood, who inspired her book *The Snow Bear*. She also shows photos of the pets she had when she was growing up.

Sometimes children dress up as their favourite characters from Holly's books. Holly has her very own special hat, based on a large Victorian hat from her "Maisie Hitchins" detective series. It is covered in feathers and flowers and even has a peacock hiding among the decoration!

At the end of each event, Holly always makes time to answer children's questions, sign books and pose for photos with her fans. The queues often go out of the bookshop door!

Holly also likes to keep in touch with her fans through her website. Here, she shares exciting news about upcoming books and has a page where fans can leave her a note and share their favourite things about her books. You can visit her website: www.holly-webb.com

A SHAGGY DOG
TALE

"So, are you ready for the surprise? Let's go out into the garden, then."

"But it's raining!" Milli looked up at her mum in surprise, and Ben nodded.

"Raining," he echoed. Then, "Ooh, can I take my umbrella?" Ben was only four and he loved the rain – waving his umbrella about and splashing in puddles. Milli wasn't as keen.

"I know it's raining." Mum looked out of the window. "But never mind. Dad and Grandad will be waiting for you. They were up really early this morning sorting it out."

Milli looked around the kitchen, wondering what sort of surprise it could be, and if Dad had left anything lying around that might give her a clue. But there was nothing, except a bag of dog food sitting on the counter. Mum must have bought it for Grandad's spaniel, Coco. Grandad lived in the next street – his garden actually backed on to Milli and Ben's – and Mum often picked up shopping for him.

"Oh, Mum." Milli shook her head. "You got the wrong kind again. You'll have to take it back to the pet shop and explain. You know Coco doesn't eat the puppy kind any more."

Mum stared at the bag, her eyes widening slightly. "Oh yes. Oh dear," she muttered.

"Don't worry," Milli told her. "Mr Biggs will change it, won't he? He did the last time you got it wrong."

"Silly me!" Mum smiled. "Anyway, are you nearly ready? Dad said to send you out as soon as you'd finished breakfast."

"I've finished," Ben said at once, pushing away a plate of uneaten toast. "I don't like toast any more."

Mum eyed him for a moment – she knew quite well he only ever ate toast for breakfast, but clearly the surprise in the garden couldn't wait.

Milli bolted down the last of her cereal and stood up, glancing out of the window. It was so unfair that it had to rain on the first day of the holidays.

She loved the sound of a surprise, and of course she didn't want to spoil things for Dad and Grandad, but did they really have to do it now? She guessed it was some sort of treasure hunt. Dad had done a brilliant one in the Easter holidays, with a big chocolate egg each as the prize. Maybe if they didn't go now the clues would get all soggy. Ugh, they probably already were.

Trying to feel excited, Milli followed her little brother into the hallway and put on her wellies and raincoat. Ben was burrowing in the cupboard under the stairs for his much-loved umbrella.

It had been Milli's once, and it had a handle in the shape of a dog's head and little dogs all over the fabric. Milli still loved it, too, but Auntie Grace had given her a new umbrella for her birthday, and she supposed the dog one was a little bit babyish now. Especially for someone who didn't even have a dog.

At least they sometimes got to play with Coco. She was gorgeous, and Grandad let Milli and Ben come out for walks with him and Coco all the time.

It just wasn't quite the same as having their own dog, that was all. Whenever Milli mentioned getting a dog, Mum and Dad always said, "Oh, but you've got Coco!" They hadn't really though. Milli hardly ever got to feed

Coco, and Coco had never slept on her bed.

She didn't even sleep on Grandad's bed, only in her basket in the kitchen, which Milli thought was a real shame. Why have a dog and not let it snuggle up on your feet at night? But Grandad said it was bad training.

"Come on, Milli!" Ben called impatiently. "The surprise!"

Milli hurried after him as he raced out into the garden, struggling with his umbrella. She helped him put it up and they gazed around, wondering what they were supposed to be looking for. Mum nodded helpfully towards a large pot of geraniums, and Milli blinked at it. The flowers were all pink, but there was something white sticking up in the middle of them. A clue!

"It is a treasure hunt! Are we going all the way into Grandad's garden, like at Easter?" Milli asked Mum, but her mum only smiled.

"Read the instructions!"

Ben pulled the white card out of the flowers. "Look, Milli, it's a dog!" It was – a cardboard cut-out of a dog. It had a sweet, hairy face – such long hair that its bright black eyes were almost hidden. It was a photo of a real puppy, Milli realized, not a drawing like she'd first thought.

"It's an Old English sheepdog," Milli told Ben. "Like my dog-shaped slippers."

Ben nodded. "All furry," he agreed. "What do we have to do? Is there chocolate?" he added hopefully.

"I don't know, but I bet there's a prize."

She ducked under Ben's umbrella, half-crouching so she could see what was written on the back of the dog picture.

"Can you read the instructions? Have they run?" Mum asked anxiously from the kitchen door.

"Only a little bit," Milli told her. "I can still read them."

Ben tugged Milli's arm. "What does it say?"

Milli read it out to him. "'Please help me find a new home, and pick up all my belongings on the way.'"

"What's 'belongings'?" Ben frowned.

"It means the puppy's things," Milli explained, smiling excitedly. She'd caught the treasure-hunt bug now, even though Ben's umbrella wasn't big enough for the both of them and there was rain dripping down inside the sleeves of her anorak. They set off down the path.

"I bet Grandad came up with this. He loves dogs just as much as we do. We have to look for things that might belong to a dog. Um, like a lead. Or a dog basket."

"A snail?" Ben asked, pointing at a large, stripy snail crawling across the path in front of them.

"Don't be silly," Milli started to say, and
then she stopped. It looked like the snail had a
big red arrow painted on its shell in nail polish!

"But which way are we supposed to go?"
Ben asked. "The arrow's moving!"

Their garden had lots of little paths
running between the flowerbeds and Mum's
vegetable patch, so there were a couple of

different ways they could take.

The snail was pointing left. But had he
started off that way round? Milli crouched
down and stared at the damp path. There was
a twirly silver trail, looping round and round.
It looked like the snail was a bit confused.
Probably Dad had moved him to fit into the
treasure hunt and he'd thought the snail would
just stay put. Milli traced it back carefully, and
then pointed towards the bird table.

"That way!" she told Ben dramatically, and
he raced off.

"Yes, yes, Milli, look! A bowl!" She
reached up on to the bird table and carefully
brought out a blue china bowl with "DOG"
written on it. "And there's another arrow,"
Ben reported, "stuck to the side of the bird

table. It's pointing towards the swing."

Milli nodded slowly as she looked carefully at the bowl. She didn't recognize it – unless Grandad had got a new one for Coco, and Dad had borrowed it for the treasure hunt.

On the seat of the swing was a cut-out photo of a blue padded dog basket. Another arrow led them to the greenhouse, and inside, dangling from one of the tomato plants, was a lovely bright red collar, with a lead attached. Had Coco got a new lead, too?

"What else does a dog need?" Ben asked, handing the collar and lead to Milli. "Oh, food!"

Milli coiled up the collar and lead

inside the bowl, her eyes widening. She
was remembering the bag of puppy food
Mum had left on the kitchen counter. Dogs
needed food, Ben was right. And Mum
wouldn't really have mixed up the bags
again, would she? *Please help me find a new
home*, the instructions said. Milli's heart
thumped. A new puppy would need special
puppy food. What if it wasn't just
a game?

Then again… Milli sighed. Mum was
scatty sometimes. That was all. "Food," she
agreed, looking round for another arrow,
and then she laughed as she spotted one cut
into the side of a cucumber, pointing out of
the other door of the greenhouse, towards
the gate in Grandad's fence.

Dad and Grandad had put in the gate a couple of years before, when Ben and Milli and their parents had first moved into the house. It meant they had an extra-long garden to play in.

Coco came racing up to them as they  opened the gate, her long ears flapping. She seemed very excited, and she nuzzled them lovingly. Then she shot away again, whooshing round the rosebushes, barking loudly.

"We haven't found the dog's home, yet," Ben pointed out, waving to Dad and Grandad, who were sitting on the bench on the patio, sharing an enormous umbrella.

"We found a basket," Milli said doubtfully.

"That's not a home, that's a bed," Ben said firmly. "The dog has to have a house."

Milli looked over at Dad. He was smiling, as though he agreed with Ben.

"I can't see any more arrows." Milli checked the gate, to see if there was an arrow stuck to the other side, but there wasn't. Then suddenly she laughed, and turned Ben so that he was facing down the garden, looking at Grandad's neat little square of lawn. It was usually neat, anyway. The grass was much longer than it normally was, and mown into it was a big arrow – pointing straight to the bench, where Dad and Grandad were waiting.

"Are you the prize?" Ben shouted, racing towards them. "Are we going on a trip? Are you taking us somewhere?"

Then he spotted the box at their feet. He peered at it and nodded triumphantly.

"I guessed it! There's a picnic in that box, isn't there, Dad?"

But the box was a big cardboard one, with handles at the top. Too big for a picnic.

"No. Guess again." Dad smiled. "What do you think, Milli?"

Milli looked down at the picture of the basket, the bowl, and the collar and lead.

She didn't want to say what she was hoping, in case everybody laughed, and told her of course the prize wasn't a dog. But the big cardboard box beside the bench was wriggling, just a little bit, and Coco was sitting next to it now, sniffing it excitedly. Grandad gathered her up on his knee.

Dad was laughing. "I think Milli's guessed. Why don't you open it?"

Ben frowned. "But we missed a clue," he burst out. "I think we did it wrong. We never found the house for the dog."

Milli knelt down next to the box. Carefully

she opened the flaps, and looked inside. She gave a gasp and smiled up at Dad, and he nodded encouragingly. Very gently Milli lifted out a little grey and white tousle-furred puppy.

The little dog had a long, shaggy fringe over his eyes. He was peering out from under it, looking shyly up at Milli and Ben.

"I think we did," she whispered.

"He's going to live in our house?" Ben asked, staring at the puppy in amazement, and slowly stretching out one hand to pat him. The puppy licked his fingers, and Ben squeaked excitedly.

Milli nodded, snuggling the puppy against her, and hoping he didn't mind the rain. *"Please help me find a new home,"* she reminded Ben of the first clue. "And we have. He's really ours."

Holly's Pets

Holly has owned many pets over the years. Here you can meet a few of them.

Alice out for a walk

Name: Alice

Breed: English Bull Terrier

Favourite food: Anything she could steal!

Likes: Nicking tissues out of people's pockets

Dislikes: Sandy paws, we always had to carry her at the beach

Name: Rosie

Breed: Tabby

Favourite food: Cheese and onion crisps

Likes: Sleeping somewhere warm

Dislikes: Being put in a cat basket

Rosie trying to
camouflage herself
with the carpet

119

First day
with Sammy
and Marble

Marble and
Sammy sleeping

Name: Marble and Sammy — they were brother and sister
Breed: Tabby
Sammy's favourite food: Tuna fish
Marble's favourite food: She'd eat anything!
Sammy likes: Nicking mushrooms and chasing them
Marble likes: Sleeping
Sammy dislikes: Moving house
Marble dislikes: Being woken up!

Milly in the
kitchen sink

Name: Milly
Breed: Bengal
Favourite food: Ham
Likes: Getting into places she shouldn't
Dislikes: Pigeons daring to fly into her garden

Milly in the
cupboard

LEO'S GREAT ESCAPE

"Can we go to bed now, Mum?"

"But, Will, it's only four o'clock!" Mum laughed. "And I'm afraid Father Christmas won't come until you're *both* asleep."

Mum and Will both turned to look as a small, sparkly whirlwind blew through the kitchen. Will's little sister Hattie was wearing three tutus, one on top of the other, her favourite pink wellies, and a tiara. She was waving a light-up fairy wand that played "Twinkle, Twinkle, Little Star", but she was singing "Jingle Bells" loudly enough to drown it out. Under her other arm was Susie, the family cat. Susie was looking quite worried. She was used to Hattie treating her like a teddy bear, but Hattie was being a bit madder than usual today.

Will looked back at Mum, his eyes round with panic. "What if she never goes to sleep?"

Mum gave him a hug. "Don't worry. If we can stand the singing for another half an hour, she'll probably fall asleep on the sofa." She glanced down at the table. "What are you making, Will?"

"A Christmas stocking for Leo." Will held up a paper stocking shape.

"Won't he just eat it?" Mum asked gently.

Will rolled his eyes. "Yes, Mum! That's the point! What do hamsters like doing best?"

"Chewing holes in things." Mum frowned, thinking of the school library book that Will had left too close to Leo's cage. She had had to apologize to his teacher for the chewed-up edges, and it had been very embarrassing. Leo was a champion chewer. His cage lived beside one of the windows in Will's bedroom, and Will's spaceship curtains had a line of little holes along the bottom, too. Will said they made the curtains look nicer.

"Exactly," said Will. "And eating. So I'm not going to colour it in, I'm making little holes in it, and I'm going to push sunflower seeds and peanuts into the holes. Those are his absolute favourites."

"Very clever. Have you made a Christmas stocking for me, too?" Mum asked.

Will frowned. "Mum, you're far too old for that."

Mum sighed. "I'll just have a mince pie then. Do you want one?"

"I hate mince pies – they taste all brown." Will shuddered.

"I'll have one." Dad came in, looking a bit stressed. "And I need some coffee." He filled the kettle. Dad had been hiding in the living room with the door shut, wrapping presents. Everyone had been banned, and he'd even put a chair in front of the door after he caught Hattie and Will peering through the keyhole. "We've run out of sticky tape."

Will grinned to himself. That sounded promising! "I'm going to go and give Leo his Christmas stocking," he said, pushing in the last sunflower seed. "I bet he'd like a mince pie, Mum."

Mum shook her head. "Uh-uh. He's fat enough as it is."

Will ran upstairs to his room, opening the door carefully and making sure that Susie and

Hattie hadn't followed him. Hattie loved Leo, and always wanted to hold him. But Will worried that she'd accidentally squeeze him too tight – or even worse, that she'd drop him and Leo would disappear somewhere in Will's room.

Susie loved Leo, too – but for all the wrong reasons. Susie thought Leo was a snack on legs, and she seemed to think that Will was just fattening Leo up for her. Perhaps even as a Christmas present.

Will was very careful every time he got the hamster out of his cage. His cousin Josh had a pet mouse called Smartie, and he'd let Smartie out once to explore his model Star Wars spaceship. It had taken three days and trails of sunflower seeds all over Josh's bedroom before Smartie was back in his cage.

"Hey, Leo! Look what I've got for you…"
Will opened the cage door, and there was
a flurry in the corner of the cage as Leo
wiggled himself out of his bedroom. It was

stuffed full of
bedding, and the
door was quite a
tight fit for Leo
anyway. Eventually
he popped out, and
pattered over to

the door like a little walking snowball. Leo
was a white hamster, and very fluffy.

Will put the stocking inside the cage,
and Leo looked at it interestedly, sniffing at
the peanuts. Then he seized one in his sharp

little teeth, and pulled it. It didn't want to come. This time, Leo gave the stocking a determined tug and dragged the whole thing back into bed with him.

Will grinned as Leo's fat white bottom disappeared into his bedroom. He could hear rustling and little satisfied hamster noises. Leo seemed to be enjoying his present. Then he jumped up as Dad yelled from downstairs. It sounded as though something bad had happened – Dad sounded really cross.

Will made for his bedroom door, anxious to see what was going on. He didn't want anything happening to spoil Christmas.

"Hattie, you have to wait until tomorrow! It's not Christmas Day yet!"

Dad was in the hallway, crouching down next to Hattie, who was holding a large present. A large, half-unwrapped present, with the corner of an interesting box poking through…

As he heard Will coming down the stairs, Dad grabbed the present and put it behind his back. "Stop right there!" he told Will. "Hattie went present-hunting, but she opened one of yours. I need to wrap it up again. Right, you two. There's a good film starting in a minute. Just go and watch it, please! And don't come in the living room until I've finished wrapping this up again. Sorry, Will. I'm going to have to hold it together with string…"

Hattie fell asleep watching the film with Susie on her lap, and Will felt pretty sleepy, too, by the time it was finished. He didn't mind going to bed a bit early – the sooner he was asleep, the sooner it would be Christmas Day.

But as he climbed the stairs to his room, he was suddenly wide awake again.

His bedroom door was open. He *never* left it open!

He thought quickly back to the last time he'd been upstairs. He'd given Leo his stocking. And then he'd heard Dad telling Hattie off and gone down to see what was going on. Will suddenly felt cold – and it was nothing to do with the snow falling outside the landing window.

Had he shut Leo's cage?

Leo's Great Escape

Will raced up the last few steps and burst into his room. Then he let out a howl of horror. The cage was wide open, and a few scraps of bedding were scattered on the window seat.

Will checked every corner of the cage just in case, but he knew that Leo wasn't there. He was out. Somewhere in the house – he could be anywhere!

Mum had heard him shout, and hurried into his room. "Oh, Will! He hasn't escaped, has he?"

Will nodded miserably. "And my door was open," he whispered.

"Oh no!" Mum looked horrified. She didn't mind Will having a hamster, but she certainly didn't want one in her bedroom.

Dad put his head round the door. "Did I hear that right? There's a runaway hamster on the loose?"

Will frowned. Dad seemed to be making a joke of it. "What if Susie eats Leo?" he sniffed. He was trying not to cry.

Dad's eyebrows shot up. "I hadn't thought of that! Don't worry, we'll shut Susie in the kitchen. So your bedroom door was open then?"

"Yes!" Will wailed. "I ran downstairs when I heard you telling Hattie off, and I forgot to shut it!"

"Ah!" Dad looked round, as if he hoped Leo would just run past. But there was no little snowball shape trotting along the landing.

But there *was* a cat. Susie had appeared silently, a black shadow creeping up the stairs. Now she was sitting on the top step, looking smug. Her whiskers looked particularly long and shiny – the whiskers of a very well-fed cat.

"Maybe she's eaten Leo already," Will whispered in horror.

"I'm sure she hasn't," Mum said, hugging him. "Don't worry, Will. We'll all look for him. He can't have got far."

But Will thought she didn't look too sure.

It had never taken Will so long to get to sleep on Christmas Eve before. He kept sitting up to peer at the special Leo-catcher he'd made out of a tall biscuit tin, a pile of books and an awful lot of sunflower seeds. But there was no hamster in it. They'd looked everywhere. Dad had pulled out all

the furniture to check under it, and Hattie
had almost capsized the Christmas tree
trying to see if Leo had gone to sleep in the
tinsel.

Will twitched as he heard a little pattering
sound. His heart raced with hope. Were those
little hamster feet?

Then he sighed. Just a branch tapping
against the window.

Every time he turned over, Will was sure
he could see Susie's eyes gleaming in the
dark, as she waited to pounce on Leo. Mum
had shut Susie in the kitchen as soon as
she'd appeared outside Will's door, but Susie
was sneaky. Will wouldn't put it past her to
escape somehow – if it meant a hamster for
Christmas supper.

He felt so guilty. What if he never saw Leo again? Christmas was ruined. He didn't even care what was in that huge parcel any more.

Will lay there, staring at the empty cage and the dark night sky outside.

"Please, Father Christmas," he whispered to the stars, "when you come down our chimney, if you see a hamster anywhere..."

Will was deep in a dream of Leo squeaking in horror as a dinosaur pounced on him, when he realized that the squeaking was actually Hattie. She was bouncing on him.

"Wake up! Wake up! I want to open my stocking!"

Will groaned. And then smiled. Christmas morning! Presents!

Then he remembered. His stomach dropped, just like it did in the lift at the shopping centre, and it was as if his heart really was sinking, like they said in books.

"There's lots of things in yours!" Hattie told him excitedly, peering over the end of his bed.

Will nodded. Mum had made him hang up his stocking just before bed last night, even though he said he didn't want to – that all he wanted for Christmas was Leo back. Safe and sound, and all in one piece.

"You've got a chocolate Father Christmas!"

Hattie frowned. "I haven't. That's not fair. And you've got a furry thing."

Will didn't really care what was in there, but he didn't want Hattie unpacking his stocking for him, which she was obviously about to do. Besides, he was curious. A furry thing? He wouldn't have thought Father Christmas would bring him a soft toy.

He hauled the stocking on to his lap, and looked inside.

Then he smiled. There was a little white fluffy snowball nestled next to the chocolate figure. Very gently, Will wriggled his hand in, and scooped Leo out of his hiding place. The snowball snuffled sleepily, opened one beady little black eye to stare up at Will – and went back to sleep.

Father Christmas hadn't brought Will a teddy.

He'd brought him back Leo.

HAMSTERS

These little balls of fluff were
originally discovered in the desert,
but now live in lots of countries
all over the world.

FACTFILE

Animal Group:
Mammal (rodent)

Size:
Varies depending on breed

Colour:
Black, brown, grey, white, golden, cream

Personality:
Friendly and active

Food:
Fruit, vegetables and cereals

Did You Know?

Hamsters don't have very good eyesight.

The largest breed of hamster can grow up to 34cm long — that's bigger than some small dogs!

Hamsters rub themselves against objects they pass in order to leave a scent trail that will guide them home.

Famous Hamsters

Babs In the festive film *Second Star to the Left* Babs the hamster helps to return a lost Christmas present to Santa Claus.

Rhino From the Disney film *Bolt*, this TV-obsessed furball helps Bolt the dog find his way back to his owner after he ends up lost in New York.

Holly's Writing Tips

Read!

By reading lots of different books, you'll learn what makes a fantastic story.

"It's important not just to read things you know you will like, but to try different sorts of books."

Be Inspired!

Inspiration is everywhere. Perhaps you overhear an interesting conversation, see a beautiful landscape or meet a fascinating person.

"Lots of the animal stories I write are based on things that really did happen. Most of the books link back to a true story."

Listen!

A good way to make your story feel real is to think about people you know.

"Try and imagine how your characters would feel — sometimes you can almost act out their conversations in your head — that really helps!"

"Do we have to put this one up, Mum? It's really tatty." Lily held out a little furry ornament shaped like a kitten. It *was* tatty. It'd had whiskers once, but they were long gone, and the tip of its tail was missing, too. The pink bow round its neck was grubby and frayed.

"Oh, we can't not have Tiggy!" Mum exclaimed, taking the little ball of greyish fur and looking down at it lovingly. "You made this for me, don't you remember? You and

your dad made him together, from one of those
sewing kits, when you were about, ohh, five?
You were so proud of him, and you named him
Tiggy."

Lily sighed loudly, but she was smiling.
"OK, OK. But please can we put him round
the back? Now we've got all these
new glittery decorations, he doesn't
really fit in."

Mum reached
up and hung
Tiggy the kitten
on the tree,
over to one side
out of the way, with a silver glitter snowflake
right in front of him. You wouldn't have seen
him at all, if you didn't know he was there.

The Christmas Cat

Lily went to bed early on Christmas Eve, much earlier than usual. She wanted it to be Christmas as soon as possible, even though it was going to be a strange one. For the first time, she wouldn't have her dad with her for Christmas Day. He was stuck in Scotland, where he'd had to go for a work trip. He should have been back yesterday, in plenty of time for Christmas, but the heavy snow had closed the airport.

Dad had been really upset when he phoned. "I'm sorry, Lily. I've tried the station, but none of the trains are running either. They said maybe on Boxing Day. I can't believe I won't be there to spend

Christmas morning with you and your mum."

Lily couldn't believe it either. It seemed worse because she had been so happy about the snow! She loved snow, and she'd gone out with all the other children from her street, and they'd had a snowball fight, and made a snowman – it was still there, on her front lawn. But then that same snow had stopped her having Christmas with Dad.

Perhaps it was because she had gone to bed so early that she woke up early, too. Her bedroom was still totally dark, and her alarm clock said it was only half past five. Half past five! Mum would be really grumpy if Lily went and woke her up now.

The Christmas Cat

She wriggled one foot further down under her duvet and poked experimentally at the end of her bed. Yes! Her stocking was definitely full. She turned on her bedside light to have a look. Mum wouldn't mind her unwrapping a few of the presents. She'd save a couple to open with her later.

Her stocking was full of fun things — a new purse, some sweets, some really cute new slippers, and a couple of books. She could nibble a bit of chocolate reindeer and read for a bit — but she just didn't feel like it. Lily sniffed. It felt really wrong for it to be just her and Mum at Christmas. Why did Dad have to go and get himself stuck in the snow?

Suddenly, Lily climbed out of bed, slipped her feet into her new slippers, and pulled on her fleece. She wasn't going to lie there and be miserable – she was going downstairs. She could get some juice or something, curl up on the sofa for a bit. She crept down the stairs, and sneaked into the living room. It was dark down here, too, and cold. Lily turned on the Christmas tree lights, and watched them twinkle, shining on all the beautifully wrapped presents underneath. She didn't feel any more cheerful, and the tree looked spooky in the greyish morning half-light.

Lily sighed, and then something strange caught her eye – what looked like a spider's web on the Christmas tree. She reached up to pull it away, and then realized that it was Tiggy, that scruffy little ornament she and Dad had made.

Lily took him down carefully, and curled up on the sofa. She'd pretended to Mum that she didn't really remember making him, but of course she did. And she'd have been upset if Mum hadn't put him up, too.

Lily had always been into crafty things, even then, and Gran had given her the kit so she could make something for Christmas. Lily stroked Tiggy's balding head, and smiled, remembering her and Dad sitting at the kitchen table, Dad patiently threading the big plastic sewing needle for her again and again.

She had talked all the way through, about how she wished Tiggy was a real cat – grey, with brownish stripes and bright green eyes. The eyes in the kit were shiny green beads that you had to sew on, and amazingly enough, Tiggy still had both of them.

Lily had told Dad all about Tiggy's favourite food – tuna sandwiches, just like her, and how he'd sleep on the end of her bed at night. Dad had laughed, and said that a real cat wouldn't let her dress him in a pink bow like that one.

Lily stared down at Tiggy's grey fur sadly. She'd always wanted a cat. But every time she asked, Mum and Dad said, "When you're older." Looking down at the big lopsided stitches that held Tiggy's green glass eyes on, Lily felt her own eyes sting, and a tear ran down the side of her nose, closely followed by another and another. Some of them soaked into Tiggy's stripy fur fabric.

"Sorry," Lily muttered, stroking them away. He was nice to stroke, even if he was tatty.

The Christmas Cat

Afterwards, Lily was never sure exactly
when Tiggy changed. She wasn't really
concentrating, just stroking the tiny cat
without thinking about it. Until she wasn't
stroking a furry ornament, but a great big
stripy tabby cat, stretched out blissfully
across her whole lap and falling off both sides.
He only had two-thirds of a tail – just like the
little ornament.

Lily stopped stroking him in shock, and
the cat half rolled over in a lazy way, and
waved a fat stripy paw at her. *"Prrp?"* he
asked, politely but clearly telling her
to get back to stroking, please. Lily
obediently ran her hand down his back,

noticing that he was one of those gorgeous tabbies with a furry line down his spine and masses of thin stripes, like fishbones.

She gave a little giggle, wondering if he'd like a tuna sandwich, and the cat leaped off her knee, purring loudly, and looked eagerly towards the kitchen.

The Christmas Cat

Almost sure now that she must be dreaming, Lily followed the cat to the fridge. She found half a tin of tuna and dolloped it generously on to a couple of slices of bread. The cat sat at her feet and mewed hungrily. Lily cut the sandwich in half and put it on two plates, which she placed on the kitchen table.

The cat immediately jumped on to a chair, and stared at her expectantly. Oh well. Mum would say it was unhygienic, but this was only a dream, so it didn't matter. Lily and Tiggy ate their sandwiches – Tiggy licked the plate, but Lily didn't – and then he stepped delicately on to Lily's lap.

Lily yawned. It was only six o'clock.

She stood up, her arms full of slightly fishy-smelling cat, and padded back to the sofa, curling up against the cushions. The cat walked round her lap about seventeen times, and finally settled himself in a tight, neat ball, head and tail tucked in. Then they both fell asleep.

Lily's mum woke her up two hours later, laughing.

"What are you like, Lily! A tuna sandwich for breakfast, on Christmas Day! We'd bought those yummy chocolate croissants, don't you remember? Why didn't you wake me up?" She sat down on the sofa next to her and gave her a hug. "Happy Christmas, Lily. We'd better wait a while to ring Dad – I bet he'll still be asleep."

Lily blinked up at her, feeling dazed. Where was the cat? Oh – of course. It had been a dream. Her eyes filled suddenly with tears again, and she looked down at her empty lap miserably.

Mum peered at Lily's top, looking surprised. "Lily, what have you got all over your fleece? It looks like cat hair. Have you been playing with that cat next door?" She brushed at the front of Lily's top.

But the cat next door was black and white, and these hairs were silver-brown tabby. Lily looked up at the Christmas tree, and Tiggy was up there again. But he wasn't tucked away at the back any more. He was hanging right in the middle, where everyone could see him, and he didn't look quite as tatty as before. He looked like a very contented tabby cat, full of tuna fish.

Holly's True-life Tales

Here are my top four tales of things that really happened to my pets...

The Sandwich

This was my dad's desperate attempt to stop our English Bull Terrier, Alice, jumping up at the table. She was a terrible thief. He made a sandwich filled with mustard, chilli sauce, pepper, curry powder and everything else he could find in the kitchen cupboard that would taste disgusting, and then he left it temptingly on the edge of the table.

Alice came in, checked that no one was looking (we were all hiding at the other end of the room to see what would happen) and grabbed the sandwich, taking it under the table to eat.

We expected whining, pawing at her nose, that sort of thing. Instead, she wolfed it down, and jumped up again to see if there was another of these yummy sandwiches... My dad gave up.

Alice the sandwich thief!

The Singing Dog

Our other dog, Max, a wire-haired dachshund, used to join in when my brother played the clarinet. He would sit next to the music stand and howl. This is where I got the idea for Sam's trick, barking "Row, row, row your boat", in *Sam the Stolen Puppy*.

The Stag Beetle Hunter

Our new cat, Milly, has decided it's too boring (or too much hard work?) to hunt mice or birds. So far, her total haul is one frog and three stag beetles. But at least one of the stag beetles fought back and got her with its pincers, which I think she deserved...

This is Milly!

The Mushrooms

My husband and I adopted two kittens from the Cats' Protection League when we moved into our first house — Sammy (Sampson, named after the cat in the "Church Mice" books by Graham Oakley) and Marble (named after cake).

Sammy was obsessed with mushrooms. He would steal them from the kitchen table — a paw would appear and whisk the mushroom away. Then he'd go mad chasing the mushroom round the kitchen, until he'd shredded it, leaving a small pile of slimy mushroom bits for you to stand on. I've never met another cat who does this.

This is Sammy!

THE
DISAPPEARING
DUCKLINGS

"I know it's the Easter holidays, Lara, but it's still really late." Lara's dad shook his head. "You're definitely not watching TV when we get home. It's bedtime."

Lara sighed. "OK. I suppose I am quite tired after all that shopping and our huge tea!" Lara and her dad had been out for the day, shopping for new school uniform, and then the cinema for a treat. It had been a beautiful warm spring day, but now it was just getting dark and the streetlights were coming on.

Lara yawned, then peered through the windscreen. "Hey, Dad, what's that?"

"Oh no, not something run over?" Lara's dad braked gently. "I can't see anything; whereabouts are you looking?"

"On the pavement on our side of the road. I think it's a duck!" Then Lara gasped. "It's Polly! And she's got ducklings with her, too! Oh, aren't they gorgeous?"

Lara's dad pulled the car over to the side of the road, and they stopped to watch, laughing as the little ducklings scurried along after their mother.

The Disappearing Ducklings

The mother duck, Polly, was a smart, plump mallard, with neat, shiny brown feathers. Lara had fed her and the other ducks in the pond at the local park many times when she and Dad had gone there for walks. She was sure it was Polly – Lara recognized her from the extra big purply-blue flash on her side.

"I haven't seen her in ages! I wonder what she's doing so far from the pond?" Lara said.

"Maybe she didn't want to lay her eggs somewhere as busy as the park, and now that the babies have hatched, she's taking them back home."

Lara nodded, then gave a little gasp. "But Dad, if she's going to the park…"

179

Her dad was already undoing his seat belt, a worried look on his face. "Yes, she's going to have to cross the road, isn't she. Oh look, she's stepping off the pavement already. She'd better be quick – the cars really speed round that corner up ahead." He opened his door and got out of the car.

"Be careful not to scare her, Dad," Lara said, climbing out of the car, too. Polly had hopped down into the road, and was looking up and down the street with her head thoughtfully on one side.

"I think she knows it's dangerous," Lara's dad murmured, as they stood watching. "She's probably quick enough to get across safely, but the babies might not make it.

I don't think we can stop them though –

ducklings always follow their mother…"

One by one the little yellow and brown ducklings hopped and tumbled down the edge of the kerb, all cheeping anxiously. The mother duck set off across the road, quacking as if to encourage them, and all seven babies followed her in a long, wavering string.

Lara made to follow them into the road, but her dad caught her hand. "No! For a start we don't want to frighten them, and I'm not having you messing around in the middle of a busy road. Stay where you are!"

Lara hovered on the kerb, her eyes fixed on the feathery fluffballs in the middle of the road. Then she looked up sharply – there was a car coming!

The car sped round the corner towards

Polly and her babies.

Lara jumped up and down on the pavement, waving, and Dad started to step into the road to stop the car, but the driver didn't seem to notice – he simply sped past, narrowly missing the ducklings.

"He didn't even see us! Oh, Dad!" Lara couldn't bear it – she had to do something. She grabbed her dad's hand, glanced quickly up and down the road to make sure no more cars were coming, then dashed across, dragging Dad with her.

"Lara, careful!" Dad muttered, but Lara could tell he was anxious about the ducklings, too.

The mother duck was already on the opposite kerb, quacking angrily. Obviously the car rushing past had really scared her.

The ducklings, however, were milling about on the edge of the road, making frantic little squeaking sounds.

"They can't get up on to the pavement," Lara whispered, crouching by the kerb, just a couple of metres away from the wriggling mass of ducklings. "Can't I help them up, Dad? Would it scare them too much?"

"Let's not risk it unless we have to," Dad murmured. "Birds are really fussy about how their babies smell – it's part of the way they tell which ones are theirs. If the ducklings smell strange because we've left our scent on them, Polly might abandon them. Oh no, look!"

The biggest of the ducklings had tried to hop up on to the kerb, fluttering and scrabbling, but it fell straight back down again.

Lara's dad automatically reached out a hand, and then drew it back, sighing. "It would be so easy for us to help the poor little thing up!"

"I don't think Polly wants us to touch them," Lara whispered back. "She's giving me a really funny look!" The mother duck had retreated to the fence on the far side of the pavement, and she was glaring at Lara and her dad. "We're trying to help," Lara promised, but Polly simply stared at her with beady reddish-brown eyes, and made an anxious quacking noise.

Dad looked round. "Uh-oh. There's another car coming… Stay where you are, ducklings!"

This car raced past, too, and the ducklings went into a panic, rushing about and cheeping frantically. Suddenly, the biggest one, the one that Lara was sure had been first in line after his mum, just disappeared.

"Where did he go?" Lara gasped. She scanned the kerb, struggling to see clearly in the dim light. Then she heard a strange, echoey cheeping noise. "Oh no! Dad, he fell down the storm drain!"

"Are you sure?" Dad replied. Then they watched in horror as the other six ducklings solemnly hopped through the gap at the edge of the storm drain grating, and

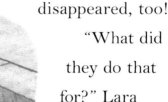

disappeared, too! "What did they do that for?" Lara wailed. "The first one fell in by accident, but the others just followed him!"

A chorus of unhappy squeaks and cheeps echoed out of the storm drain, as the ducklings discovered that they were trapped.

Dad sighed. "Well, funny human smell or not, we're going to have to help them now. There's no way they'll be able to get out of there on their own." He edged slowly along to the grating, trying not to scare the mother duck. She was hovering worriedly in the middle of the pavement now.

"This must lift up somehow…" Dad gripped the edge of the grating and tried to haul it up. "*Oof.* Hang on, I'll go and get the tyre jack out of the car – see if I can lever it up that way." He got to his feet and looked at Polly, who had crept closer to the drain and was keeping a beady eye on Lara. "Don't worry," he murmured soothingly to her, "we'll get them out…"

As Dad dashed across the road to the car, Lara and Polly stayed by the drain, peering anxiously down at the dark water and the babies swimming unhappily around.

"That water looks horrible," Lara said, shuddering.

Dad came back with a metal rod that Lara recognized as a tool that he had used to change a flat tyre once. "Hopefully I can use this to pull the grating up. I've brought the torch from the car, too. Point it at the grating for me, Lara." He poked the rod into the gap between the kerb and the grating, and Polly hissed worriedly, backing away.

"He's helping, really he is," Lara promised her.

Just then, the heavy metal grating eased up slowly and creakily. "Well done, Dad!" Lara shone the torch down into the murky hole beneath, and Polly fluttered her wings anxiously.

"I hope she doesn't follow them in," Dad muttered. "She looks like she might nip me if I tried to lift her up! OK. Here goes." He leaned down over the hole, lowering his hand into the water. A moment later, he gently scooped out one of the baby ducks, putting it down next to its mum. Lara smiled as the duckling huddled close to Polly, cheeping.

Meanwhile, Dad continued with his rescue mission. "Two… Three… Come on, you, don't wriggle! Four *and* five. Where are the other two?" Dad put his head closer to the hole. "There were seven, weren't there, Lara?"

Lara nodded. "I'm sure there were." She carefully counted the ducklings, who were now all lined up along the kerb, watching the rescue. "There must be two more somewhere."

Suddenly, Dad cocked his head, listening carefully. "They're in the pipe," he groaned. "I can hear them squeaking. I don't think I can reach them, though. It's a pretty tight space."

"I've got smaller hands – shall I try?" Lara asked.

Dad looked at her doubtfully for a moment, and then nodded. "But be careful. Here – let me hold the torch."

Lara passed the torch to her dad, then leaned over the hole and reached her hand inside.

It smelled horrible, but she didn't mind. She hated to think of those two little ducklings, scared in the dark pipe.

Even so, she shivered as she put her hand

into the greasy-looking water.

"I can feel one, I think!" she gasped, and pulled out a damp little bundle of fluff. Carefully, she placed the dazed-looking duckling next to its brothers and sisters. Then she looked back down into the drain and laughed. "The other one's followed him out!"

The last duckling was paddling and splashing around in the main drain hole now, cheeping loudly. The other ducklings seemed to know that he was the last one of them to be rescued, and they all chirruped loudly, too.

Smiling delightedly, Lara scooped up the last duckling and popped it down on the kerb.

Dad and Lara grinned at each other and got to their feet. As they watched Polly fussing over the babies, padding around them and checking that they were all present and correct, Lara caught her dad's hand and glanced up at him proudly before looking back down at the little family.

"Aw, it seems like they're getting ready to

head off," Lara cooed. "See you soon, Polly! Dad, can we go to the park tomorrow and check they're OK?"

Dad smiled. "Definitely. Bye, ducklings!"

Then Polly led her babies off in a long line again, all looking rather damp and dirty, and they slipped through the fence into the long grass, on their way home to the pond in the park.

DUCKS

Everyone has lots of fun visiting ducks at their local park, but how much do you really know about these fascinating feathery creatures?

FACTFILE

Animal Group:
Bird

Size:
Various

Colour:
Black, white, grey, brown, cream, green

Personality:
Busy and practical

Food:
Grasses, insects, small fish. (Bread is actually not very good for ducks!)

Ducks have a waterproof outer layer of feathers. Even when a duck dives under the water, its lower layer of feathers stays dry.

Ducklings are already fairly advanced when they hatch. They are born with their eyes open and learn to run and swim quickly.

A female duck will line her nest with feathers plucked from her own body to make it cosy for her eggs.

Famous Ducks

The Ugly Duckling The main character from the fairy tale by Hans Christian Andersen, the little duckling is bullied by his peers for being different. But it turns out that he is really a swan — the most beautiful of all the birds!

Jemima Puddle-Duck This silly duck gets herself into all sorts of trouble in a story by Beatrix Potter. Jemima sets out to find a place to lay her eggs, but a fox convinces her to make a nest in his den! Fortunately, a friendly dog rescues her and she escapes the fox's hungry jaws.

197

Holly Around the World

Holly's animal books have been translated into thirteen languages, including Finnish, Vietnamese and Russian.

From Hong Kong to Poland, Holly has travelled all over the world to meet her fans from other countries.

"I really love speaking to children from other countries about my books as they often have very different experiences of reading them than children do here in the UK. I'm always very excited to talk to them and find out what characters they love and whether their backgrounds alter the way they read the stories. I also love talking to children about what they enjoy reading in general. I find that really exciting – and useful as well."

Most of the names in Holly's stories have to be translated to make them more familiar in other languages. For example, Buttons the chocolate Labrador from *Buttons the Runaway Puppy* is called Czarus in Polish — unfortunately, the 'chocolate buttons' joke doesn't translate! Fluff, from *Lost in the Snow*, is called Flöckchen in German translations, Pusię in Polish and Pörrö in Finnish!

Children and their families come from all over to visit Holly at a reading or signing. Sometimes they bring piles of her books that they've read, or scrapbooks about their favourite characters.

JUST IN TIME
FOR CHRISTMAS

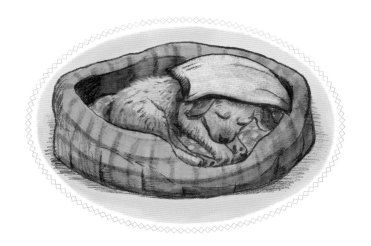

"I hate this time of year," one of the girls at the shelter sighed, as she opened the door on to the exercise run, and four excited dogs shot past her. They were barking so loudly they drowned out the carols on the radio in Reception.

"Christmas?" Her friend Lucy stared at her. "How can you hate Christmas, Kate? That's awful!"

"Not everything about Christmas…"

Kate stopped talking to glare at one

of the dogs racing about outside, and he slunk away from the smaller dog he'd been squabbling with. "But when the shelter closes on Christmas Eve, it just makes me feel so sad, thinking of all the dogs shut in here on Christmas Day. I know they get a special lunch and extra treats, and I've bought them all some rawhide chews. But it isn't the same. They ought to be with a family for Christmas. Or anyone, really. A proper home of their own."

Lucy made a face. "Now you've got me all miserable, too." She sighed. "Well, we've got a few more days to find this lot the perfect home."

A little later, Max the terrier-cross came in from the run with his eyes sparkling.

Just in Time for Christmas

It was his favourite twenty minutes of the day.

The run was a big fenced-in area, where a few dogs could be let out at a time, so they had a chance to really stretch their legs. The dogs in the shelter didn't get a lot of exercise. There were a few volunteers who came and took them out for walks, but never enough, and there were lots of dogs in at the moment, and not very many people rehoming them. It was such a busy time of year – hardly anyone wanted to get a new dog just before Christmas.

Everyone at the shelter was hopeful about Max, though. He was so sweet – very young, not much more than a puppy, and he had short golden-brown fur, big soulful dark eyes, and enormous ears that looked like they were really meant for a dog a couple of sizes bigger than he was. And Max was friendly, too – so surely someone would want to take him home?

"You know, I thought you were going the other day," Kate murmured to Max a couple of days later, as she scratched his ears through the wire of his pen, and he leaned against it, his eyes blissfully closed. "That man really liked you. I suppose he did take Buster, and Buster had been here for ages. But I wish you could have a proper home before Christmas, Max."

Max gave her hand a lick. "It isn't likely to
happen now, though," Kate added sadly. "It's
Christmas Eve. We're open, but I don't know if
we'll get anyone coming. Oh, there's the phone.
Maybe someone wants to come and visit, after
all." She dashed off to Reception to answer it.

Max yawned, and settled down in his

basket for a sleep. He didn't mind the shelter as much as some of the dogs, who scratched and whined all the time. But he did wish they got more time to run about. His first home had been with an old lady, Mrs Jarrett, who'd got him for some company. She'd loved having him, but she wasn't really able to look after him properly, and so he'd ended up in the shelter.

He'd liked it best at his old home when Mrs Jarrett's grandchildren came round and played with him. His favourite was Maisie. He liked the boys, Josh and Jayden, as well, especially when they played football with him. But Maisie was so good at cuddling him, and scratching his ears and the itchy bit under his chin. He loved to snooze with his head in

Maisie's lap. He wished he could see Maisie again. Every time he heard a girl's voice among the visitors to the shelter, he would look for her hopefully, but she never came to see him.

He buried his head under the cushion in his basket, and tried to remember how it felt when Maisie hugged him. He slept, his paws scrabbling every so often as he dreamed. Football. Chasing around Mrs Jarrett's garden. The children giggling as the ball went into a big patch of purple flowers, and they had to get it out quick before Mum or Gran noticed. He was dashing up and down the garden after them, barking at the ball. Then back into the house for a drink of water, and some of his favourite treats from the

shiny bag in the cupboard. He could hear
Maisie laughing as he gobbled them down,
and he whined in
his sleep, missing
her all over
again.

"Hey, Maxie…"
Max wriggled
blissfully as the dream-Maisie stroked him,
and called his name.

"Max!"

Max shook himself blearily, and pulled
his head out from under the cushion. Was it
food time again already? Or perhaps he was
getting an extra walk? He looked up to see
who was outside his pen.

Then he leaped out of his basket and

threw himself at the side of the pen, barking
and barking like a mad thing.

It hadn't been a dream! Or not all of it.
Maisie really had been calling his name.

"Oh, Mum, look, he remembers us!" Maisie
knelt down next to the wire pen, and Max
licked her cheek lovingly.

"He really does." Her mum sounded
surprised.

"I've missed you, Maxie," Maisie told him.
"Mum says she's sick of me moping round the
house."

"Crying all the time," Josh put in, as he
tickled Max under the chin. "We've missed
you, too, Max."

"So if we take turns feeding you, and
walking you, and we promise to clear up any

mess, Mum says we can take you home!" Maisie beamed at him.

Max looked back at her hopefully. He wasn't sure what she was saying, but from her voice, it seemed to be a good thing. Maybe she was going to take him for a walk?

Kate was smiling down at him, and she had a lead in her hand – his old lead, blue with paw prints on. He recognized it. Mrs Jarrett had given it to the shelter when she brought him in, with all his other things in case they needed them. Josh was holding his old basket and food bowls, too, Max realized, his ears pricking up.

Were they taking him back home?

"Bye, Max! Happy Christmas!" Kate

hugged him, and she was crying and smiling at the same time. "I put your Christmas dog chews in your basket," she called after him, as he walked out of the shelter, with Maisie holding his lead, sniffing at the cold winter air.

"It might snow tonight," Jayden said, as they hurried through the streets.

Max was walking close to Maisie, not wanting to let her go. She nearly tripped over him a couple of times. "Do you think he's cold?" she asked her mum worriedly.

But her mum smiled. "No, I think he's just glad he's got you back. He's such a sweet little dog. You were right, Maisie. We should have taken him home with us before."

Maisie nodded. Mum had said it wasn't a good idea to visit him at the shelter, because it would make her sad. It was actually nicer than she'd imagined, but no dog could really like it there. "Nearly home," she whispered lovingly to Max.

Max looked around him curiously. This wasn't his old home. There were more trees in the road, and lights everywhere, sparkling and flashing and changing colour. The house they stopped at had little white lights wrapped round a tree in the front garden.

The front door opened, and Maisie's dad was there, grinning. "You got him! Wow, he's bigger. Hello, Max!"

"He won't get bigger than this, honestly," Maisie told him.

Dad hugged her. "I'm not changing my mind, Maisie, don't panic. It's great to see him again."

Max stared around the hallway, his tail twitching just a little. The house smelled good. He followed the children as they trooped into the kitchen, and Josh put his basket down by the radiator, and his bowls next to it. Maisie took off his lead, and hung it on a hook by the back door, as though it had always belonged there.

Then she picked him up – she could only just manage, now he was bigger – and carried him into the living room to see the Christmas tree.

"Look, Max! Isn't it beautiful?" She nuzzled her cheek into his fur as he nosed one of the glittering decorations. "But not as beautiful as you. You're home, Max! And just in time for Christmas."

DOGS

Often called a man's best friend,
this animal is a very popular pet.

FACTFILE

Animal Group:
Mammal (Canine)

Size:
Various

Colour:
White, brown, black, grey, golden, cream

Personality:
Loyal and loveable

Food:
Meat and vegetables. Dogs can
be vegetarian

220

Did You Know?

A dog can hear sounds at four times the distance a human can.

A dog's noseprint is unique. It can be used to identify them, just like a human's fingerprint.

The most popular female dog names are Molly and Maggie and the most popular male dog names are Max and Jake.

Famous Dogs

Gromit The pet dog of inventor Wallace, Gromit is often underestimated by his owner — but he generally has a much better idea of what is going on than Wallace does! He enjoys playing chess, knitting, reading the newspaper and cooking.

Nana This loveable character from J.M. Barrie's book *Peter Pan* looks after Wendy, Michael and John before they fly away to Neverland.

221

Holly's Favourite Books

"The Chronicles of Narnia" series by C.S. Lewis

This series of seven books is set in a fantasy world full of mystical creatures and magic. The stories are about ordinary children from our world who are transported to Narnia. They help protect the Narnians from evil.

"I think I liked these books so much because of the talking animals. My absolute favourite was Prince Caspian because of the fabulous Reepicheep (a large talking mouse). I also liked the bear who sucked his paws — I sucked my thumb as a child and I suppose I sympathized!"

The Box of Delights
by John Masefield

In this story, the young hero Kay Harker is given a box with magical powers. With it, the owner can time travel, change size and fly. Kay has lots of adventures trying to keep the amazing box from getting into the wrong hands.

"This book inspired me when I was writing *The Snow Bear*, but what annoyed me about it was the ending. The journey turns out to have been all a dream, and I thought this was disappointing. When I wrote *The Snow Bear* I wanted that magical journey to be somehow real."

THE
GREENHOUSE
KITTEN

"Sophie, can you pick me some tomatoes out of the greenhouse?"

Sophie looked up from the little vegetable patch where she was weeding around her pumpkin plant. It had four baby pumpkins on it. She wanted at least one of them to get big enough to make a lantern for Halloween. It seemed a long time until then, but they were still only the size of satsumas, so there was still a way to go.

Sophie went to the kitchen window. "How many should I pick?"

Her mum held out a bowl. "Just a few to have in a salad for lunch. Thanks!"

Sophie ran down to the greenhouse.

It was a really hot day, and Mum had told her to leave the door open after they'd watered the plants early that morning. She gasped – it was steaming hot inside, even with the door open. The warmth wrapped itself round Sophie like a damp blanket.

It was like a tiny patch of thick jungle in their garden. The tomato plants were huge, even taller than Sophie, some of them. She loved picking tomatoes, searching under the hairy green leaves for the glowing red fruit. There were lots today – it had been so hot, they were all ripening up, scarlet and glossy.

Sophie crouched down to get at a particularly juicy-looking tomato, and gasped again. Staring out at her between the leaves was a small, furry face.

Sophie was so surprised that she nearly fell over. Whatever it was that was hiding behind the tomato plants seemed to be surprised, too. The little face disappeared, and there was a scuffling noise and a shaking of leaves as the creature darted away into the furthest corner of the greenhouse.

Sophie sat back on her heels and stared after it. She had only had the tiniest glimpse, but she was sure – almost sure – that it had been a kitten. There had been round, bright green eyes, a little pinkish-brown nose, and a great moustache of white whiskers. What on earth was a kitten doing in their greenhouse? Who did it belong to? Sophie was pretty sure that none of their neighbours even had a cat. She would have noticed. She knew every cat on the way to school, and their owners. She loved all the cats so much that Mum and Dad had told her that maybe they could have one of their own some day. But they hadn't said when.

As Sophie watched, the tips of those white whiskers shimmered out from between the tomato leaves. Sophie squeezed her fingers together excitedly. She had sat still enough! The kitten was coming out!

Very slowly, the rest of the whiskers appeared, and then the tips of two reddish-brown ears, with the tiniest little furry tufts on them, like a wildcat.

Sophie and the kitten stared at each other silently. Then the kitten shook itself a little (Sophie could tell, because the tomato plants shook, too) and padded delicately out into the middle of the greenhouse.

He was possibly the prettiest kitten Sophie had ever seen. He was mostly ginger, with a white chest and the greenest eyes. Even

greener than Alfie's, her gran's cat. Sophie
went round to Gran's every Thursday after
school, and Gran said that Alfie was a little
bit Sophie's, too. He adored her, and she
always brought him cat treats.

"Oh… He's lovely," Sophie whispered.

"I suppose it would be all right to give him a little bit of leftover chicken," Mum said. "He *is* beautiful. The chicken was going to be your lunch…"

"I don't mind!" Sophie said quickly.

"Mum, if he's a stray – could we keep him? You did say maybe we could have our own cat one day, and this kitten's come and found us. It's like he wants to be ours."

"I don't know, Sophie." Mum shook her head. "He must belong to somebody. What if we start thinking he's ours, and then we have to give him back to his real owner? It would be so sad."

"I suppose so." Sophie sighed. "But what are we going to do with him? How do we find out where he belongs? Oh! Maybe he's got a microchip, like Alfie! We could take him to the vet to check."

"Yes, maybe. And even if he hasn't, the vet could tell us what we should do.

I wonder if we could tempt him into a box with some chicken?" Mum said thoughtfully. "I'll go and find one."

Sophie watched sadly as Mum went back to the house. "I wish you'd disappear, just for a little while, so we wouldn't be able to take you to the vet," she told the kitten. He was nosing at her fingers now, his front paws up on her knee. "I don't want to find your owners at all. But I suppose they're missing you."

The kitten looked up at her as she crouched, and then sprang into her lap, purring a little.

Sophie gaped at him. She hadn't expected him to do that at all. "Oh, you're so friendly. You're gorgeous," she told him, stroking him very gently down his back. She wriggled herself into a sitting position, so she could cuddle him properly, and the kitten snuggled happily into her arms.

Sophie was enjoying stroking the kitten so much that she had hardly noticed her mother was away for much longer than it would take to find a box. Sophie didn't even hear the phone ringing, she was too busy crooning compliments to the kitten, and listening to his deep, throaty purr.

But eventually her mother came back up the path with a saucer of cold chicken, and

Sophie noticed that she looked quite stunned. "What's the matter?" she asked. "Couldn't you find a box?"

"I didn't look… That was your gran on the phone," said her mum, placing the saucer on the floor. The kitten took a flying leap off Sophie's lap, and began to wolf down the chicken.

Sophie giggled. "He looks as though he hasn't eaten for days!"

Her mum nodded. "He might not have done. He's been gone for five days, apparently."

Sophie stared at Mum. "How do you know?"

Mum smiled. "Gran told me! She always knows everything. This kitten belongs to a lady in Gran's reading group, who lives down the end of her road. Her cat had kittens, and a ginger one escaped out of the front door when she went out to pick up her milk. She's quite elderly, and she couldn't catch him. She left food out, and put up notices, but he didn't come back. She was telling Gran all about it at reading group last night. Gran was ringing to say keep an eye out for him!

She thought you might spot him, the way you know all the cats round here." Mum chuckled. "She was quite surprised when I told her you'd already found him… It has to be him, surely?"

"Yes." Sophie smiled down at the kitten, but her eyes were full of tears.

"I suppose we ought to go and give him back. Can he finish the chicken first?" She sniffed.

Mum crouched down next to her.

"He can. And then maybe we ought to buy him some cat food. He must be starving."

Sophie frowned at her. "What do you mean? Won't his owner have food?"

"I'm sure she does. But your gran's ringing her up right now, to say we've found the kitten, and that we'd like to keep him.

She needed to find homes for all of her kittens anyway, Sophie. And like you said – he found us."

"Really?" Sophie felt like bouncing up and hugging her mum, but she didn't want to scare the kitten. He had finished the chicken now, and was climbing back into her lap. It took a bit of effort – his tummy was a lot rounder than it had been before.

"Really. Look, I've brought my mobile – do you want to call Dad and see what he thinks?"

Sophie nodded, but she looked worried. "Do you reckon he'll say yes?"

Mum smiled. "He might be a bit surprised. But I think so." She handed Sophie the phone, and Sophie listened anxiously to it ringing. The kitten twitched his ears curiously at the noise.

"Dad! I'm in the greenhouse, and I've found a kitten in the tomato plants, and the lady who lost him wants to find a home for him, so can we keep him, pleeeease?"

There was silence for a moment on the other end of the line, and then Dad said, "Run that past me again, Soph?"

"He's a lost kitten. But Gran knows who he belongs to, and he needs a home."

"In the greenhouse?" Dad still sounded confused.

"No! With us, silly." Sophie giggled. She could tell from Dad's voice that he was going to say yes.

"And Mum says we can have him?"

Sophie looked at her mum, and held the phone out, her eyes pleading.

Mum spoke to Dad. "He is gorgeous. And it seems like we're meant to have him. I know it's sooner than we planned … mm-hm." She smiled down at Sophie. "Dad says you'd better call him Tom."

"So we can keep him?" Sophie gave a shaky little sigh of relief. "But why Tom?" She looked down at the kitten, stretched out and purring on her lap.

Her mum grinned at her. "Short for tomato."

Sophie rolled her eyes. "Trust Dad."

Mum tickled the purring kitten under

the chin. "Why don't you see if he's happy to come inside?"

Sophie gently slipped her hands round Tom the kitten, and cradled him against her shoulder. And then she carried him down the path, to go and see his new home.

An Interview with Holly

How and when did you decide to write your first book?

It was almost an accident that I started writing! I came up with a series idea in an editorial meeting whilst I was working at a publisher's in London. The plan was to work on it, and then suggest it to an author. But I realized I'd fallen in love with it when I'd named all the characters and their pets... So I decided to write it myself!

What's your favourite thing about being an author?

The best feeling is hearing from people who've read the books. It's lovely when people write and tell me about their favourite characters and animals. I remember being so involved with my favourite characters in books when I was little — it thrills me that this is happening with my books now!

When you're not writing, what sorts of things do you enjoy doing?

I spend a lot of time playing with our Bengal cat Milly — she's very lively and has heaps of energy!

You often write about magic in your books. If you could have a magic power, what would it be?

Talking to animals, because I would love to know what they think. I had a grumpy English bull terrier called Alice when I was growing up — she and I used to go on long walks when I was a teenager, and it would have been wonderful to be able to talk to her properly. Although I should think she would have been very bossy...

Where is your favourite place to write?

I have a lovely purple armchair in a tiny room that used to be the back half of our garage.

What inspires you the most?

Most of my animal stories are based on my own cats and dogs, or stories other people tell me. For example, I went to a school where a little boy told me about his mum's dog who used to climb out of the window and follow her to school! I used this as an idea for my book *The Missing Kitten* — though I changed the puppy to a cat.

Which book are you most proud of?

I think it would probably be *Lost in the Snow*, which is the first animal book that I wrote. I really love that book — the mother cat was named after the cat I had when I was a child and so it's really special to me.

MIA AND THE
LOST PENGUIN

"I'm so sorry you can't come, Mia." Mum tucked the duvet round me gently. "Dad will look after you, though. Just call if you need anything, won't you."

I made a gaspy, rattling noise – that was all I could manage at the moment.

"Oh, yes. Well, just thump on the floor, and he'll hear that."

Mum looked down at me worriedly, but then my big sister Sophie yelled up the stairs.

"Mum, we'll be late! The theatre won't let us in if we're not there on time!" Mum gave me an apologetic smile and hurried out, leaving me sniffing miserably.

It was so unfair. It was Christmas Eve, and I had the world's worst cold, and I was missing our special Christmas treat, going to see *The Nutcracker*. I love ballet, and I'd been looking forward to it for ages. But I couldn't really sit in the theatre coughing and blowing my nose and putting everybody off the wonderful story and the dancing and the costumes – oh, it was just so unfair!

Mum had said to try and sleep, but I didn't feel tired. She'd left loads of new books from the library, and Sophie had even lent me the TV from her bedroom, but I didn't feel like that, either.

I was too miserable. I flumped over on to my side, grumbling as I coughed again, and hugged Ferdie, my old toy penguin. I've had him since I was about two, and he's my best thing. I love penguins, I have loads of posters of them, and I was wearing my blue, fluffy penguin pyjamas.

"You all right, Mia?" Dad popped his head round the door. "It's started to snow, look! We're going to have a white Christmas!"

I wriggled up on to my elbow and peered across to the window. He was right. Fat, lazy snowflakes were floating down against a dark-grey sky. It had been so cold that the snow was bound to settle as well. Great. All my friends would be out making snowmen on Christmas Day, and I'd be stuck inside, if Mum even let me get out of bed.

As I lay there dreamily watching the whirling snowflakes, with Ferdie tucked under my arm, it got colder and colder. At first I thought it was just because I could see the snow falling and it was making me feel cold, but then I realized I could see my breath puffing out in front of me. I sat up, pulling my duvet round my shoulders like a big, warm cloak.

Then suddenly Ferdie wriggled under my arm, his grey feathers silky-soft. I looked down in amazement, and he gazed back shyly with his bright, beady eyes, his head on one side. Then he wriggled out of the duvet, and hopped clumsily down on to the snow, still looking back at me as though he wasn't quite sure what I was.

I shook myself, trying to wake up. I had

to be dreaming. I still had my blue penguin pyjamas on, and I was all wrapped up in my duvet, but my bedroom had disappeared. Instead, I was in the middle of a snowfield, surrounded by white, as far as I could see.

I stared around me, blinking at the brightness of the shining snow. The wind was shrieking in my ears, and flurries of snowflakes swirled around me, making me shiver. It looked as though a storm was just blowing over. I glanced over my shoulder, and gasped – huge, snow-covered mountains were rising behind us, back where I'd stupidly thought my bedroom would be waiting. I shook my head slowly, and took a deep breath of freezing cold air. Meanwhile, Ferdie was waddling clumsily away across the whiteness.

"Hey! Stop!" I jumped up, not wanting to lose the only thing I knew in this strange world, and Ferdie looked back at me hopefully. He waggled his flipper, as if to tell me to hurry up, and carried on lurching across the hard-packed snow. I followed him, skidding and sliding, and tripping over my duvet.

"This has to be a dream," I murmured, looking down at my bare feet stepping over the Antarctic snow. "If it was real, my feet would have probably turned blue and fallen off by now…"

Ferdie seemed anxious. It was clear that he wasn't just going for a walk, he was trying to get somewhere. He was only a chick, and he shouldn't really be out on his own – he should be with his parents or the other penguin chicks. I guessed he must have wandered away in the snowstorm, and got lost.

He was hopping and bouncing over the bumpy ground, flapping his funny little flippers for balance. But he didn't seem to be very good at it; he kept falling over, even though his little black feet had sharp claws to grip with. I couldn't help giggling; he looked so funny. He was so fat and furry, with his little black and white head bobbing about on top of his grey, fluffy body.

But after the third fall, I stopped laughing, or even wanting to. Ferdie could hardly get up. He seemed so tired, and he just lay down in the snow. His bright, beady eyes looked back at me sadly, and then he closed them, and he didn't move.

I caught up with Ferdie, and crouched down beside him. "Ferdie! Ferdie, wake up! You can't sleep here!" I looked round worriedly. "You'll freeze."

I was cold, and I was only a dream-person, not even really there. Ferdie might have all that gorgeous fluff, but I was pretty sure it wouldn't keep him warm for very long, if he lay there on his own in the snow.

Ferdie's eyes flickered open for a

moment, and he gave a sad little sigh, but then they closed again. They hadn't been as bright and shiny this time; they were starting to look misted over. Ferdie was giving up.

Gently I reached out to stroke him. I cuddled my toy Ferdie all the time, but this Ferdie was real, and he was wild. I didn't want to scare him. Ferdie hardly even moved when I brushed his soft feathers with my hand. Tears dripped out of the corners of my eyes, and I felt them freezing on my cheeks.

"Don't give up, Ferdie, please!" I whispered. And, hoping that I wasn't doing the wrong thing, I scooped him up in my arms.

He was a lot heavier than my toy penguin, and bigger. He smelled like fish. He wriggled a little, as though he didn't think someone should be cuddling him, but then he didn't move.

Clumsily, dragging the duvet still – I didn't want to let go of it; it felt like my only bit of home – I trailed on. Ferdie had been following a straight path. If I looked back, I could see the marks of his shuffling feet – although I hadn't left any footprints at all – I suppose dream-people don't. So I tried to carry on going in the same sort of line. Ferdie seemed to get heavier with every step I took.

At last, we came to a little rise in the snowfield, and I dragged my way slowly up it. Then I gasped. Stretched out on the ice in front of me were thousands and thousands of penguins. They were emperor penguins – I could tell because they had black heads with orange patches on the sides. That strange noise I had thought was the wind was the penguins calling to each other, loud sounds, almost like donkeys braying.

I was so excited to see them that I accidentally hugged Ferdie tight, and he made a funny little cross noise. At least he was waking up a bit; it must have been me cuddling him and making him warm again.

Then I had a horrible thought.

This was Ferdie's home, but there were at least two thousand penguins here! Which ones did he belong to? "Oh, Ferdie," I muttered to the fluffy bundle tucked inside my duvet. "I'm sure this is where you wanted to get to. But I don't know how you're going to find your mum or dad."

Ferdie was wriggling now, then he popped his little black head out of my duvet and stared around eagerly, his eyes bright and alert.

He tried to flap his flippers, and I guessed he wanted to get down, so I placed him gently on the ice, wondering sadly what he was going to do. The penguins all looked alike to me, and there were hundreds of other fluffy grey chicks, too.

Ferdie waddled down the little slope determinedly, and started to rock his head backwards and forwards, calling loudly. I could only just hear him, though, because all the other chicks were doing the same, shouting, "Piu! Piu!" again and again, louder and louder every time, and their parents were hastily trying to feed them.

I looked around, wondering if any of the other penguins would be kind enough to give Ferdie some food, but they were all looking after their own chicks. Poor Ferdie, he'd come so far, but he was still all alone.

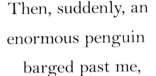

Then, suddenly, an enormous penguin barged past me, heading straight for Ferdie. He was one of the tallest ones I'd seen – he was right up to my waist, and he nearly knocked me over. He *did* knock Ferdie over, but obviously because he was so delighted to see his lost chick. He nudged him up at once, snuggled him into his tummy feathers and started feeding him.

I was colder again without Ferdie to

cuddle, so I sat down to wrap myself in my duvet. It was so cold I began to feel sleepy. The snow was falling again, those same great fat flakes there'd been outside my window at home. I wondered how I was going to get back there. *But at least I rescued Ferdie,* I thought.

He's home safe...

"Hey, Mia... Time for your medicine, sweetheart." Dad was sitting on my bed, gently shaking me. "Wow, it's chilly in here. I'd better turn the radiator up."

I blinked at him. Surely seconds ago I'd been in a snowfield full of penguins?

"Were you dreaming, Mia? You look a bit dazed." Dad smiled at me as he poured the medicine.

"Mmm." I took a quick look around. This was definitely my room.

And there was Ferdie, on my pillow. Fluffy and snuggly, smiling and safe…

PENGUINS

Penguins can't fly but their wings have adapted into flippers which propel them through the water at amazing speeds!

FACTFILE

Animal Group:
Bird

Size:
Varies depending on breed

Colour:
Grey, white, black

Personality:
Dedicated and sociable

Food:
Lots of fish!

Did You Know?

Male Emperor penguins will guard an egg for up to two months without eating while their female partners are at sea, building up their body fat. When the egg hatches, the pair swap — the female returns to look after the baby and the male leaves to find food!

Penguins spend up to 75% of their lives in the water.

Famous Penguins

Pingu This popular penguin from the hit television series of the same name lives in an igloo with his family. He often has adventures with his little sister Pinga and gets into lots of mischief with his best friend Robby the seal.

Mumble In the film *Happy Feet* Mumble the Emperor Penguin doesn't fit in with his peers — a penguin needs to be able to sing to find a mate, and Mumble can't sing at all! But he can tap dance...

275

More Favourite Books

"Sherlock Holmes" series by Arthur Conan Doyle

These detective stories were mostly written in Victorian times. The incredibly clever Sherlock Holmes solves mysteries that nobody else can crack.

"I love the way Sherlock Holmes carries out his investigations and uses tiny details to solve the mysteries. I've so enjoyed writing the 'Maisie Hitchins' stories and trying to give them a flavour of those books I adored."

A Little Princess
by Frances Hodgson Burnett

Sara Crewe attends a boarding school while her wealthy father is away in India. To begin with she's treated well, but then Sara's fortunes change and she has to adapt to a very different life.

"I particularly love the historical setting of this book — it's set in Edwardian London."

THE STORY
KITTEN

"Tell me again," Lulu begged, clutching at Martha's pyjamas so that her big sister couldn't climb off her bed.

"Again? I've already told you twice tonight, Lulu. It's time to sleep. Mum will be coming up to check on you soon. She'll be cross if we're still chatting."

"No, she won't." Lulu made a pleading face. "She might pretend to be cross, but she'll just stay and listen to the story. You know she will. It's her favourite story, too."

"Oh, all right. But just one more time."

Lulu nodded and curled closer round her sister, and Martha wriggled her feet under Lulu's duvet.

It was a freezing-cold night, and their bedroom was chilly. The wind was whistling and the weather forecast had even said that it might snow at the weekend. Not tonight, though, Mum had told them. The sky was too clear.

Martha had looked out at the stars when she'd drawn the curtains. They hung in the sky seeming close enough for her to touch, floating just beyond the branches of the old tree outside the window, caught in a net of its spindly twigs. Martha had thought she could reach out and pick a star, silver and sparkling, and make a wish on it.

The Story Kitten

"Go on!" Lulu prodded her with one finger and Martha smiled.

"One day…" The story always started the same way. "One day, maybe even quite soon, we'll have a kitten of our very own."

"To keep," Lulu added. That was important.

"Yes, to keep."

"What will it look like?"

"It will be a black kitten. Black as night. But with a little white furry star under its chin and a long black tail, with just a tiny touch of white at the end."

Lulu nodded happily. She knew all this. Martha must have told the story a hundred times by now. But Lulu loved to hear it. Her big sister made it sound so certain. So true. "And we'll call him Sam," Lulu said. Both Lulu and Martha thought Sam was a gorgeous name for a cat. "Will he sleep on my bed?" she asked dreamily.

"Yes, most nights," her sister agreed. "Sometimes he'll sleep on my bed instead. Maybe Mum's bed, too, every so often."

Lulu nodded. That was fair. "And he'll play with us?"

"Yes. We'll have to get him some cat toys. One of those feathery things you wave up and down. And a wind-up mouse to chase."

"But Lucy at school says her cat never

plays with his proper toys. He just steals bits of Lucy's brother's Lego, and chases that all over the house." Lulu frowned. "Maybe we should buy some Lego instead." She was silent for a moment and Martha wondered if she was falling asleep at last.

"Martha, how will we get the kitten?"

Martha frowned. They hadn't thought about that before. Somehow, their beautiful black and white story kitten was too special to have come from a pet shop, like any ordinary cat.

"He'll find us," Martha decided. "On a moonlit night, full of stars, just like tonight. We won't know that he's coming. He'll walk straight through the night. And it will be so dark that no one will see him as he goes past. Except for the little white tip of his tail, so it will look like a tiny white star floating by."

"Will Sam be OK, travelling all on his own?" Lulu asked anxiously. "He's only a very little kitten."

"Yes, but he's an adventurer. I should think he's had lots of adventures already." Martha thought for a minute, and smiled. "He's been a witch's kitten, but all those spells made him sneeze, so he had to give that up. And then he was a ship's cat on a pirate ship. But he got sick of nothing but fish to eat. He loves fish, of course. But he likes a change occasionally."

"Smoky bacon crisps," Lulu murmured sleepily. "They're my favourite, too. Did he ever get seasick?"

"Yes, a little bit, just like you. So now he wants to settle down and find a forever home in a house that doesn't sway up and down."

"I just wish it wasn't so dark…" Lulu murmured.

"But dark's good for a black kitten," Martha reminded her. "And he can see perfectly in the dark, too."

Lulu suddenly sat up in bed. "What colour are Sam's eyes?" she asked excitedly. "I've forgotten."

Martha knew that she hadn't really. The kitten's eyes were one of Lulu's favourite parts. "They're green," she reminded her sister. "But not a bright green. A soft blue-green, like the sea. Maybe because he did some of his growing up on a pirate ship," she added. "His eyes are like the sea round the treasure islands."

"Perhaps he really is coming tonight…" Lulu suggested, her eyes shining. She pulled the duvet up to her chin and stared hopefully at Martha. "Where is he now?"

"I said a moonlit night, Lulu. That's all. A night *like* tonight. Not actually, really tonight."

"But it could be," Lulu said stubbornly. "It could be tonight. Couldn't it?"

The Story Kitten

"I suppose so," Martha sighed.
She snuggled her cold toes further in,
underneath the backs of Lulu's knees, and
closed her eyes. She loved this story, too,
but she had told Lulu about the kitten so
many times now. She just wished it was all
true. Or that they could have any everyday
cat. She wouldn't mind if it wasn't their
little black story kitten. She would love a
tabby cat, or a ginger. A white cat, even. She
wouldn't care if the kitten that turned up
was purple, to be honest, as long as it was
theirs.

Mum had said that they could have a cat
one day, when they were a bit older. But she
never said when. Martha sighed and Lulu
prodded her again.

"Where is he, Martha? Where's Sam now?"

"Just walking towards school. He's come all the way across the fields and through the bluebell wood."

"Through the woods! What about the foxes? And the badgers?" Lulu squeaked. She had been for walks in the woods and they had seen the badger holes. They looked big.

"He slipped past them all. Some of the time he went through the trees, jumping from branch to branch and tree to tree, like a squirrel. And even if a fox did try to chase him, his claws are needle-sharp and he fights like a pirate. He probably has a spell or two still hidden in those whiskers, as well. There might be a really confused fox

"Ummm. He'll climb the tree." Martha nodded towards the window. It was still windy and the branches were tap-tapping against the glass. It was a spooky sort of noise, but the girls were used to it.

"I can hear him!" Lulu stared wide-eyed at the window. "Mewing! Didn't you hear, Martha?"

"That's the wind. Sam's just a story, Lulu. One day we'll have our own cat, but this one's just a story kitten."

"It was him," Lulu said stubbornly. She pushed back the duvet, and climbed out of bed. "You'll see."

Martha sighed, and followed her little sister to the window. Lulu was hesitating, her fingers on the curtains, as though she didn't

quite dare to pull them back. She wanted to
believe so much — she didn't want to see just
the darkness, and the tree...

Martha put her arm round Lulu's
shoulders and drew the curtains open. "You
see," she said. "I'm really sorry, Lu." The
wind mewed, louder and louder, and Martha
shivered.

But Lulu had frozen next to her. "Look,"
she whispered. "It's him. Just like you said.
Oh, Martha! He's come."

Martha looked out of the window, her
heart thumping so hard she felt dizzy.

Balanced on the spindly branch was a
small black kitten, with a white-tipped tail,
mewing loudly and rather crossly now, as if
to tell them to hurry up and let him in.

Blinking, Martha turned the key and
pushed the window open. The kitten
stepped daintily down the branch and
jumped on to the sill. His black fur was
ruffled with the cold, but his sea-green eyes
were shining. He rubbed his head against

Lulu's cheek and peered mischievously up
at Martha.

"Just like you said," Lulu whispered
again, as she gently wrapped her arms
round the little black kitten and cuddled
him. "You came all that way, Sam. Martha
said you would. Oh, Martha, you're so
clever."

"I wished," Martha murmured. "I wished,
and he came."

CATS

These warm bundles of fur have made purr-fect pets for thousands of years.

FACTFILE

Animal Group:
Mammal (Feline)

Size:
75cm from tip of tail to tip of nose

Colour:
White, brown, black, grey, golden, cream

Personality:
Independent and confident

Food:
Meat and fish

Did You Know?

Cats spend around 30% of their lives grooming themselves.

A cat can jump up to five times its own height in a single leap.

Cats can make up to 100 different sounds — dogs can only make about 10!

Famous Cats

The Cheshire Cat This peculiar puss from Lewis Carroll's *Alice's Adventures in Wonderland* can vanish into thin air! Sometimes he'll leave behind his grin — a very strange sight!

Puss in Boots This fashionable cat from the traditional fairy tale is cunning and clever. He uses his wits to help his master get rich and marry a beautiful princess.

Other Titles by Holly Webb

My Naughty Little Puppy

A Home for Rascal
New Tricks for Rascal
Playtime for Rascal
Rascal's Sleepover Fun
Rascal's Seaside Adventure
Rascal's Festive Fun
Rascal the Star
Rascal and the Wedding

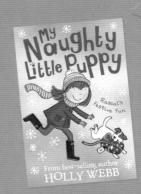

Maisie Hitchins

The Case of the Stolen Sixpence
The Case of the Vanishing Emerald
The Case of the Phantom Cat
The Case of the Feathered Mask
The Case of the Secret Tunnel
The Case of the Spilled Ink

Animal Stories

Lost in the Snow
Alfie all Alone
Lost in the Storm
Sam the Stolen Puppy
Max the Missing Puppy
Sky the Unwanted Kitten
Timmy in Trouble
Ginger the Stray Kitten
Harry the Homeless Puppy
Buttons the Runaway Puppy
Alone in the Night
Ellie the Homesick Puppy
Jess the Lonely Puppy
Misty the Abandoned Kitten

Oscar's Lonely Christmas
Lucy the Poorly Puppy
Smudge the Stolen Kitten
The Rescued Puppy
The Kitten Nobody Wanted
The Lost Puppy
The Frightened Kitten
The Secret Puppy
The Abandoned Puppy
The Missing Kitten
The Puppy Who Was Left Behind
The Kidnapped Kitten
The Scruffy Puppy
The Brave Kitten

Winter Animal Stories

The Snow Bear
The Reindeer Girl
The Winter Wolf